Fenner, Phyllis R
The hunter and the
hunted

Date Due

DATE DUE			
Q.VAL B 1 02 3 '79			
DORR M 1 0 1 9 '81			
MONTA H 1 0 2 1 '81			
MACDO L 8 85			
KLA. R. L 8 19 87			
GAZ C 1 - 1 '88			

10369

A collection of ten adventuresome tales by
such authors as London, Cloete, and Kantor
which depict the experiences of hunters and
the hunted.

THE
HUNTER
AND THE
HUNTED

Stories of Forest and Field

■

Other Collections
by Phyllis R. Fenner

■

BEHIND THE WHEEL
Stories of Cars on Road and Track

BROTHER AGAINST BROTHER
Stories of the War Between the States

CONTRABAND
Stories of Smuggling the World Over

DANGER IS THE PASSWORD
Stories of Wartime Spies

THE DARK AND BLOODY GROUND
Stories of the American Frontier

NO TIME FOR GLORY
Stories of World War II

OPEN THROTTLE
Stories of Railroads and Railroad Men

OVER THERE!
Stories of World War I

THE PRICE OF LIBERTY
Stories of the American Revolution

selected by
Phyllis R. Fenner
illustrated by CHARLES GEER

William Morrow and Company
New York

THE HUNTER AND THE HUNTED

Stories of Forest and Field

■

For
Marion Chatfield Cressey
"Friends are the nearest relations."

CONTENTS

■

SPORT
OR
WAY
OF
LIFE

■

To some, hunting means boots and hunting jackets, red caps and shirts, rifle over the arm, a cabin in the woods, deer season. But in the past, hunting represented a way of life. It and trapping were man's earliest way of getting food. When wild animals were domesticated and farming developed, hunting became a sport. Then the ability to outwit the animal grew more important than the killing.

Real hunting is a contest between the hunter and the hunted. While the hunter has a gun he doesn't have all of the advantages. The animal can run faster, knows the woods better, and has keener senses. If the hunter depended on his gun alone, the animal would win almost every time. Therefore, the hunter must know the habits of the animal he is hunting, so he can come close enough to shoot. The thrill of hunting, no doubt, comes not only from the contest but from the out-of-doors activity. It takes the hunter into the country and is a healthy antidote to the refinements of modern life.

These stories are of hunting both as a way of life and as a sport.

P. F.

THE
WOODS-
DEVIL
Paul Annixter

■■■

For the four days since his father's accident, it had snowed intermittently. The slate-black clouds of winter had banked up in the north and west. They were motionless, changeless, remote, and ridged like banks of corrugated metal. For days during this north Maine winter, the only sun the family had seen had been a yellowish filter at midday that came in the cabin window like a thin sifting of sulphur dust.

Nathan was just bringing in the night's wood, enough short logs to burn till morning; with another pile of wood chunks beside the daubed clay fireplace they would last the following day if need be. His face and ears burned from laboring in a temperature of thirty below. He was dressed in brown linsey-woolsey; on his feet were shoes of heavy felt, stuffed with coarse, gray socks against the cold. A cap of worn coonskin crowned his shagbark hair that had not been cut in many weeks. He had reached the gangling age of fifteen and a half, when the joints are all loose and clumsy. His lean face was drawn and pinched, the dark eyes sullen from overwork.

His mother sat darning a sock over an egg, rising now and then to stir the pot of mush or turn the cooking rabbit. His father lay in the cord bunk in the corner of the cabin, his injured leg raised high beneath the blankets. His gaunt, unshaven face was etched with the memory of the pain he had endured before the settlement doctor had come to set the broken bone. Worry showed in his black eyes turned up to the ceiling poles. Little food was left for the family—a bit of jerked venison in the smokehouse, a side of bacon, some beans, and meal. The Stemlines were true woodsies. They'd been eking along, waiting for the fur season. All that they ate, spent, and wore came from their traps and rifles.

Nathan went out for the final log, and the door creaked

behind him on its crude hinges. The snow in the clearing was almost knee-deep. The forest surrounded it on all sides broken only where a road cut a black tunnel through the balsams toward the settlement down to the south.

A sudden wind rose with the darkness. Nathan could hear it far off and high, a growing roar above the forest. Abruptly it snatched at the clearing, whirling the snow in eddies; the serried pine tops bent in rhythm. Because his impulse was to hurry in and close the door against it, Nathan stood for several minutes, his face straight into it, letting the cold and darkness and emptiness sink into him.

Indoors, he eased down his log and took off his sheep-skin coat and cap, baring his mop of brown hair. He sat down beside Viney, his eight-year-old sister, playing with the endless paper people she cut out of the mail-order catalogue. The wind made hollow bottle noises down the chimney, and the driven snow made a dry *shish-shish* against the log walls.

"Listen to that," said Nathan's mother. "The Almanac was right. We're due for another cold spell. 'A stormy new moon. Keep a good fire,' Father Richard says for the ninth. 'Colder. Expect snow,' it says for the tenth."

Nathan's voice had a manly note. "It's getting colder all right, but it won't snow. It's too darned cold to snow. A fellow'd soon be stiff if he didn't keep working."

"Is the ax in?" his father asked.

"Yes." Nathan fetched it and put a keen, shining edge on it with the whetstone. Then he ran a greased rag through each of the rifle barrels. He could feel his father's approving gaze on his back as he sighted through each barrel into the firelight. "Bright's a bugle," he copied his father's invariable comment.

Then he sat waiting, his hands clasped tightly between his knees, for what he knew must come.

"Nathan," his father said presently, and the boy went over and stood dutifully by the bunk. "Do you think you can cover the trapline tomorrow, son?"

"Yes, I guess I can."

He was prickling with trepidation. The wind shook the cabin door as he spoke, and he thought of all that lay up in the far pine valley—things to be felt, if not seen or heard.

"It's a long ways, I know, and it's mortal cold. . . ." His father's voice was drained and tired, and for a moment Nathan glimpsed the naked misery and worry in his mind. "But money's scarce, son. We've got to do what can be done."

"I don't mind the cold or the snow." Nathan stared down at his feet until that look should leave his father's face.

"I'll be laid up three, four weeks, maybe more. It's four days since we laid out the line. Varmints may have got most of our catch by now. You've got to go, Nathan. If you start at daylight you can make the rounds and be back by night."

"Shucks, yes." Nathan forced a smile.

When he dared lift his eyes, he saw his father's face had hardened again in coping with the problem.

"You needn't try to bring in the catch," he said. "You can hang some of it on high boughs, then reset the traps. Main thing's to find what kind of range we got in there. Later on, you may have to spend a night in the valley. Think you'll be a-scairt to sleep alone in the deep woods?"

"Not me." Nathan's tone discounted all concern, but

misgivings quickly crowded in. "Anyhow I'd have an ax
and a rifle and plenty cartridges," he said.

His father managed a smile. "Might have to sleep in
there once every week till I'm up again. So you'd best
look at that log cache we built to store traps in. It's
plenty big enough to sleep a man."

Pride filled Nathan. This was real man's work he was
detailed to do.

"You'd best eat now and turn in early," his father said,
"so's you can start at dawn."

"All right."

"You're a brave boy, Nathan," his mother said. "You're
the provider for this family now. What a blessing it is
you're big enough to cover the line while your father's
down. Last year you could never have done it."

"He's near about as good as any man now," his father
said. "Knows the woods and critters as well as I."

Young Nathan grew more stolid than usual, holding
himself against the rushing tide of feeling. He wished he
were all they said of him. Inside he was frightened whenever he thought of the Little Jackpine Valley where their
trapline had been laid out. For three days the vision of
the valley and what he had felt there had lurked before
his mind's eye, filling him with dread, even when he tried
to put his mind to something else.

Methodically, Nathan ate the man's share of food his
mother set before him on the hewn-log table. Soon after,
he climbed the sapling ladder to the small quarter loft
where he slept. He lay quiet, pretending to sleep, but
long after the lamp went out he was still grappling with
his thoughts. Storm gripped the cabin. The snow crept
up against the walls and the night was full of voices.
Once far in the forest a wolf howled. Nathan's skin

prickled and his two hands made fists underneath the blankets.

Now and again he could hear his father stirring and knew that he, too, was thinking the same thoughts.

Dawn had not yet come when Nathan descended the ladder. He built up the fire, made coffee, and ate a hurried breakfast. He took down his old wool sweater to wear under his sheepskin coat.

"Make sure you don't forget anything," his father said. "Have you got plenty cartridges . . . matches? Belt ax? Bait?"

"Yes, Pa."

"Best take my rifle," his father said.

Nathan took down his father's finely balanced rifle with its curly walnut stock and held it proudly in his hands. It was a far better weapon than the old Sharps Nathan usually carried.

"I wouldn't take the sled," his father was saying. "It's heavy, and I want you should be back by night. Be right careful, won't you, son?" he called, as Nathan lifted the latch.

The cold bit deep. It was scarcely light yet in the clearing. The storm had died down in the night, and there was no wind now, but the air cut Nathan's cheeks like a razor. It was colder than anything he had ever known.

After twenty minutes of tramping he thought of turning back. His face and hands were numbing; his joints seemed to be stiffening. Each breath was agony. He snatched up some of the hard, dry snow and rubbed it against his stiffened face till a faint glow of feeling came. Then he ran for a long way—beating his arms, one, then the other, against his body, shifting the rifle, till his thin chest was heaving. Again his face was like wood. He was terrified, but he would not give up, would not turn back.

He covered the three miles to the mouth of the Little Jackpine in a daze. He did not know what he could do with his numbed hands if he did find a catch in the traps; he could not even use the rifle if the occasion arose. He would have cried had he been a year younger, but at fifteen you do not cry. He started into the valley.

The Little Jackpine lay at the foot of old Shakehammer Mountain, and through it a small stream rushed and snarled like a wildcat, its bed choked with almost inaccessible jungles of windfalls. It was an appalling wilderness.

Both Nathan and his father could read the silent speech of place and time in the outdoors, and what the valley had said to them had been vaguely antagonistic from the first—almost a warning. Nathan remembered how they had threaded the valley bottom, in single file, silent. The breeze had droned its ancient dirge in the treetops, but not a breath of it had stirred along the stream bed. The hiss of the water had created an intense hush.

He remembered how he had spat in the boiling waters to show his unconcern, but it hadn't done much good. Several times as they headed homeward, Nathan's father had stopped abruptly in his tracks to look behind and to all sides. "Queer," he had muttered. "A full hour past I had a right smart feelin' we were bein' watched and followed. I still got it."

"I had it, too, Pa," Nathan had said. "It's mighty fearsome back yonder, ain't it?"

"It ain't a bear." His father had evaded the question. "May be some young lynx cat, figurin' he'd like to play with us. A lynx is a tomfool for followin' humans."

They had backtracked to the top of a rise to look, but they saw nothing. Then the valley struck its first blow. A perfectly placed boulder that had lain poised for untold years had toppled at that exact moment to crush the older Nathan's leg as he scambled down a rocky ledge. . . .

Nathan passed the spot, but he did not pause. Something seemed to listen behind each tree and rock, and something seemed to wait among the taller trees ahead, blue-black in the shadows. After a while it felt warmer, perhaps because he was climbing. Then he came to the first trap and forgot wind, cold, and even fear.

A marten, caught perhaps two days before, lay in the set. Its carcass had been partially devoured, its prime pelt torn to ribbons as if in malice. Roundabout in the snow were broad, splayed tracks, but wind and sleet had partly covered them, so that their identity was not plain. But they told Nathan enough. Neither fox nor wolf had molested this trap, nor was it a bear. Nathan knew what it was, but he wasn't admitting it yet—even to himself.

He stood up, his eyes searching for a glimpse of a secret enemy, but the valley gave back nothing. Except for the soughing of the balsam boughs far overhead, the stillness was complete.

He moved on between the endless ranks of trees and again had the feeling of being watched. At intervals he stopped to glance back along his trail, but saw nothing. The trunks of the dark trees seemed to watch him as he approached, slipping furtively behind him as he passed.

The next trap had been uncovered and sprung, the bait—a frozen fish—eaten, and the trap itself dragged off into the brush and buried in the snow. It took nearly half an hour of floundering and digging to uncover trap and clog. Hard by was another set, and there Nathan saw a thing that made his skin crawl. The remains of a porcupine lay in the trap, and the creature had been eaten—quills, barb, and all. Blood from the jaws of the eater was spattered all around. Only a devil could have done that! Beneath a spruce he saw clearly the despoiler's trail —splayed, hand-shaped tracks like those of a small bear, each print peaked with fierce claw marks.

These were the tracks of a giant wolverine, the woods-devil, bane of all hunters and trappers.

For long minutes Nathan stood in the dusky shadows, fighting down his fear. He had heard about the evil fortune that fastens upon trappers molested by a wolverine. Then he thought of what awaited him at home that stricken look on his father's face. His fear of that was greater than his fear of the valley.

He hung his sack of frozen bait on a high bough. Useless to reset any of the traps now, for the creature he was pitted against could smell cold steel, unbaited, through two feet of snow, and, in sheer deviltry, would rob and destroy wherever it prowled.

Nathan plodded on again, his chest hollow with hopelessness, not knowing what he could do.

The snow became deeper. One after another he came upon six more sets that had been robbed. Each had held a catch, and each ravaged pelt meant the loss of food and clothing to his family.

Then Nathan gave a whimpering cry. He had come to the seventh trap, and that one had contained treasure, a pelt worth a whole season's work to the Stemlines. This was a black fisher marten, always a trapper's prize. If only he could have carried home such a pelt on this first day of his rounds! How smoothed and eased his father's worried face would have become! But the woods-devil had destroyed it—an even more thorough job than on any of the others, as if he had sensed the value of this catch.

The boy whimpered again as he crouched there in the snow. Then anger flooded him, fought back the tears. He rose and began the endless plodding again, peering into every covert for the dark, skulking shape. He did not know the size of a wolverine. He'd never seen one. He recalled old Laban Knowles' tale of the wolverine that had gnawed his walnut rifle stock in two and scored the very rifle barrel. And Granther Bates told of a woods-devil that had killed his two dogs, then gnawed through a log wall to rob him of his grub cache.

It was afternoon when Nathan neared the farthest limit of the trapline. Of twenty-odd traps, only two had been unmolested. Abruptly he came upon a fresh trail in the snow: the same hand-shaped tracks and demon claws, no more than an hour old. Grimly he turned aside to follow their twisting course.

He was descending a steep, wooded slope, when on a sudden impulse he doubled back on his own tracks and plunged up the grade through deep snow. As he reached the crest, a dark, humped shape took form beneath the drooping boughs of a spruce—a ragged, sooty-black and brown beast, some three and a half feet long, that lumbered like a small bear; it was lighter colored along its back and darker underneath, in direct contrast to all other forest beings. It saw him, and its green-shadowed eyes fixed on those of the boy beneath a tree some hundred feet away. The black jaw dropped open, and a harsh grating snarl cut the stillness. The utter savagery of this challenge sent a shiver through Nathan's body. His rifle

flew up, and without removing his mitten he fired. The
whole valley roared. In the same instant, the wolverine
disappeared.

Nathan rushed forward, reloading as he ran. Under the
spruce were several drops of blood in the snow, but the
wolverine had vanished completely. Because of his haste
and the clumsiness of his mittened hand, Nathan had
only grazed the animal; he'd lost his one big chance.

Panting, stumbling, sobbing, the boy plunged along
the trail, bent low, ducking under the drooping limbs of
the trees, sometimes crawling on hands and knees. He
saw other drops of blood. They gave him heart. He had a
lynx eye, his father had often said. He would follow on to
the very Circle if need be; he would not miss a second
time. His one hope now was to settle with the beast for
good and all.

The trail led down along the stream bed, twisting
through tangles of windfalls, writhing masses of frost-
whitened roots, and branches that seemed caught in a
permanent hysteria. Twice he fell, but each time he
thrust high the rifle as he went down, to keep the snow
from jamming its snout. He plunged on again; he did not
know for how long or how far, but he was aware at last
of the beginning of twilight. And the end of light meant
the end of the trail. Victory for the enemy.

The way had grown steeper. He was coming to the
narrow throatlatch of the valley's head, a place where
hundreds of great trees, snapped off by storm and snow-
slide from the slopes above, had collected in a mighty log
jam, a tangle of timber, rock, and snow that choked the
stream bed from bank to bank. Countless logs lay criss-
crossed helter-skelter with two- and three-foot gaps between. The great pile was acre large, fifty feet high, rank
with the odor of rotted logs and old snow.

Into this maze led the trail of the woods-devil. Nathan skirted the pile. The trail did not come out!

Trembling, he squeezed his way between two logs into the great jam. The wolverine might be fifty yards inside, but somehow it must be ferreted out. In and in Nathan wormed his body, pausing to watch, to listen, his rifle thrust carefully before him. Then down and down into the twisting chaos of dead and dying trunks, led by his nose, for the rank odor of the devil's den now filled the air. Coming upward from the very bottom of the jam, it was fouler than any skunk taint.

Nathan stopped short, his body tensing like a spring. To his ears came a harsh and menacing growl, but from which direction he could not tell. He waited but could see nothing. He loosened the safety on his rifle and wriggled forward again, and again the air was filled with that ominous challenge. This time it seemed to come from behind him. He whirled in panic, but there was nothing. His terror mounted. The creature must be watching him, and he could not see it. And might not there be *two* of them? Then a movement caught his eye, and he glimpsed a soot-dark shape in the lower shadows.

The boy wriggled on his belly along a slanting log, maneuvering for a shot through the intervening timbers. He braced himself, craning far downward. . . . Then in the very instant he took aim, he slipped on the snow-sheathed log. The gun roared; the shot went wild; and, as Nathan caught himself, the rifle slid from his ice-slick grasp. It clattered downward, striking against log after log before it lodged at the bottom of the jam, snout down in snow, its barrel clogged and useless.

In that instant all the craft that has made man master of the wild fell away, and Nathan was reduced to first principles. The wolverine clambered slowly upward. Inexorably it advanced upon him. He screamed at it, but there was no vestige of fear in the beast. Nathan's hand went to his light belt ax; he gave no ground.

With a panicking shout he leaned and swung at the low flat head, but missed because of hindering logs. He swung again and again, and the blade struck, but with no apparent effect, for the creature's advance never checked. Its small, inplacable eyes shone blue-green.

It lunged suddenly for Nathan's dangling legs. He flung himself up and over the log, then slipped on the icy sheath, grasped desperately for another log, and slipped again to a point eight feet below. He flung around with a cry of desperation, expecting to meet open jaws, as the demon was almost upon him. But the animal was logy. Its power lay in its indomitability—a slow, irresistible power.

In it came again, above him now. He stood upright, braced on two logs, to meet it. He was crying now, sobbing and unashamed.

He struck again, yelling with each blow of the belt ax, but hack and cut as he would, the beast bore in and in, maneuvering along the undersides of logs to avoid the ax blows.

Then as Nathan slipped again, he avoided the traplike jaws. He fell to the bottom of the jam, biting snow as he screamed. He was on his feet again before the creature above released its claw hold and dropped upon him like a giant slug.

Flinging an arm up over his throat, he jerked back blindly. Spread saber claws tore open his heavy coat. Then the ax fell again, blow after blow with all his strength; he shouted with every blow. No longer cries of terror, but of war.

The thing would not die. The jaws clamped on Nathan's leg above the knee, and he felt his own warm blood. Then his hand found the skinning knife at his belt, and the blade sank into the corded neck—turned till the clamp of jaws released.

Nathan climbed up out of the abatis till half his body emerged from the top of the great jam, and there he rested—panting, spent. He whimpered once, but there were no tears now. Instinctively, his eyes lifted skyward. Overhead, as night drew on, a great rift appeared in the leaden canopy of cloud, and a few stars shone through. He fixed his eyes on the brightest star until chaos left him; then his vision steadied, as if his head were higher than ever it had been before, in a realm of pure air. His brain was almost frighteningly clear.

The trickle of warm blood down his leg roused him. He pressed his heavy pants leg around his wound till he felt the bleeding stop. Painfully, he turned down into the maze of logs again and brought up the rifle. Then down again to struggle upward, dragging the woods-devil by its short and ragged scut. He laid it out on the snow and pulled out his bloody knife. He wasn't tired now, he wasn't cold, he wasn't afraid. His hands were quick and sure at the skinning; even his father had never lifted a pelt with smoother, defter hand. Darkness shut down, but he needed no light. There was no hurry. The head he cut from the body, leaving it attached to the hide.

He thought of the proud fancy that made the far northern Indians covet a garment made of a wolverine's skin. Oh, there would be talk in the cabin tonight; they would sit at the table long after their eating was done, as great folk were supposed to do. He'd recount all the details of the day and the fight before he brought his trophy in to show.

He rose at last and rolled up his grisly bundle, fur side

out, and moved away through the blackness of the trees, sure of tread, for he had the still hunter's "eyes in the feet." Reflection from the snow gave a faint light. He was limping a bit.

Off in the black woods, a wolf howled dismally, and Nathan smiled. Never again would the night dogs make his skin crawl. Never again would he be afraid of anything above ground.

THE
LAST
CHARGE
Edison Marshall

■

■■■

The house of Doctor Cruikshank, medical missionary in East Africa, stood on high ground about half a mile from a large Kikuyu village, and the windows of the dining room overlooked a wide expanse of thorn and mimosa forest and golden veldt. As the doctor, his wife, and his son, Albert, sat about the table after tiffin, the light through those windows was white-hot. Mrs. Cruikshank was thinking how it would fade her curtains. It would roughen and dull the finish of her mahogany sideboard, brought all the way from Scotland. The doctor was troubled about the crops—the rains still two months away, and the country drying up like an old bone. But Albert, aged sixteen, was simply taking in the view, with keen, calm eyes.

It was a wonderful view. Some little gray specks between here and the water hole were zebras. A dark patch under some mimosa trees in the extreme distance was very probably a herd of wildebeests, standing close in the narrow shade. If he cared to get his father's binoculars he could certainly find kongoni and topi, long-leaping 'palas and tommies with forever-whirling tails; and there was a sporty chance of giraffes or ostriches or eland or, perhaps, all three. Five times he had seen lions from these very windows, and on two occasions, buffaloes. Some day he would see what was so rare at this break in the hills, a rhino. That is, if his father did not persist in his unspeakable intention of sending him off to school.

"I won't be home for supper, but I'll have Kanano fix us a box of lunch," Albert announced to his parents.

"Another night out with that black boy, I suppose," Doctor Cruikshank grumbled. "It's all right for you to have a gunbearer, Albert, but I'm afraid you're getting too thick with him."

"Fundi always keeps his place, sir." Albert spoke respectfully, but his eyes twinkled.

"I hope so. But the sooner we pack you off to Edinburgh, the better."

True, Doctor Cruikshank thought, Albert was well advanced in his studies. Unless he chose to enter one of the professions, probably he could continue his schooling right here in Africa and turn out a well-rounded man. But he would be forever a colonial. He would miss the cultural and social advantages of university life at home. This, Doctor Cruikshank felt, must not be contemplated. He was an enlightened man and a democrat, but tradition must be served.

Albert's mother was gazing at him too. She was thinking how tall he was, how lithe and how brown. If she were a Plymouth Rock hen who had found a jungle cock among her brood, she could not have felt more surprised. His eyes were light gray like his father's, but of different setting and shape. Usually they were very quiet, but when they lighted up, it was with a full incandescence that was startling. He was homely, she thought, but in a way that glowed in her heart.

"What's the plan tonight?" she asked with a smile.

"The big black-maned lion has taken another cow from our village. Fundi and I are going to lay for him."

"I thought you didn't like to kill lions," Doctor Cruikshank broke in.

"I don't—just to be killing 'em. It's awfully exciting, but. . . ." Because he could not explain what he felt, Albert turned red. "And, Mamma, we'll be safe as Moses behind four feet of thorns."

This last was probably true, Albert's mother was thinking, but she gazed with a troubled brow at this flesh of her flesh.

"He's a grand old lion," Albert went on, "but he's gone too far."

"All right, Albert, but please be careful." She held his big, sunburned hand.

Albert began the undertaking by shooting a zebra. He liked the striped ponies, but their numbers were countless, and the flesh would not go to waste. Borrowing the mission lorry, he dragged the carcass around the village cattle kraal to make a blood trail that the black-maned raider would likely cross. Then pegging it down in a likely spot in the thorn forest, he and Fundi built a *boma*—a thorn enclosure—ten paces away. By sundown the pair were in position, with a blanket apiece, food and water in reach, their heads colliding pleasantly as they gazed through the two-foot loophole. The drama of the African night was about to begin, apparently for them alone to see.

Alone, but together. They spoke little, but occasionally turned and glanced, too happy not to communicate, into each other's eyes. The pure, radiant blue of the African sky slowly paled. The vultures, perching forlornly on the thorn trees, eyeing the bait, but afraid to trust their clumsy bodies on the shadowed ground, stood forth in grim silhouette. A herd of zebras swept by, heads up and tails waving, a picture of vital being. Only an hour before, they had dozed and grazed, but half alive, under the mimosa trees.

"We'll have good luck tonight *bwana*," Fundi whispered in the Kikuyu dialect. "Mighty luck, I think."

"I'm not your *bwana* now. You must call me that in front of my father and the villagers, because they don't understand, but we were born in the same kraal and the same month. Does Simba care whether our skins are white or black?"

"No, my brother."

"That's right. Brothers to each other, and to those out there!" Albert swept his hand toward the dim veldt.

"They are all about us, my brother. Be still, for I think some of them are coming."

The vultures had suddenly taken wing. A marabou stork, with a bill like a bayonet, swore furiously on his high perch and flapped off into the gloom. There was a moment of breathless suspense; then, from all sides, dark figures with sharply sloping backs came skulking. At once they attacked the kill as though it were a living foe, and they themselves bold beasts of prey instead of hyenas.

For the two watchers, it was a battle of shadows. The twilight had changed through ever-deeper shades of gray until it matched the moonlight, then had been spirited away. The moonlight seemed silver bright on their faces, but thin clouds strained it, and at ten paces it blurred the shape of everything, and washed out colors until the scene had the eerie grayness of a dream. But this softening of every bloody sight made the accompanying sounds seem all the more shocking. Dim shapes would meet, blend for an instant, and scatter, with movements light as tumbleweeds in the wind, but the snarls and growls and yelps and shrieks of pain revealed how deep the fangs had slashed and how cruelly the bone-cracker jaws had closed, as the hyenas fought one another over the meat. Albert and Fundi were trembling with excitement, and very lightly, ready to disengage if any job arose, they had clasped hands.

"You say we're brothers, the white man and the black," Fundi whispered.

"Yes."

"Also we're brothers of the Black Mane, and of his

brothers hunting out there, and of the horned game they
hunt?"

"That's what we believe. Maybe we're wrong."

"I believe it, brother. Then are these who've come to
dinner our brothers too?"

"They do the best they can, Fundi. They don't eat
clean food, but except for them and the vultures, the land
wouldn't be clean. Sometimes they are brave and sometimes afraid, like us, and the mothers love their cubs. But
I don't feel toward them as toward the clean beasts. I'd
kill one of them to save a fawn. I couldn't help it."

Fundi nodded contentedly. "Then eat your fill, brothers," he said in low tones to the pack. "There'll be enough
left for Black Mane."

Suddenly the uproar ceased. It was cut off as by a
sword of silence. The hyenas stood like stones in the
grass. Then one of them uttered a sharp yelp, as though
he had been kicked in the ribs, and the whole pack scut-
tled in all directions.

"Simba," Fundi whispered.

For the next half minute, the two hunters found it difficult to breathe. But it was a rapturous breathlessness,
and they felt each other very close and unafraid. Then
out of the shadows, full into the moonlight, strode three
lions. They came boldly, royally.

Albert tingled with admiration for the great beasts. He
wanted them to live on in might and glory, not lie still in
the red grass like those he had shot before he gained
understanding of his homeland. But if one of the three
were Black Mane, he had made up his mind to kill him.
Leveling his big rifle, he signaled Fundi to turn on his
shooting light.

Except for the stately raising of their heads, the lions
did not move. They were curious about the sudden and

blinding glare in their dim, silvery world, but not yet
alarmed. One of them stood with one foot on the striped
shoulder of the dead zebra. The two others were on the
opposite side of the kill, and no sculptor could have
grouped them more impressively. Albert saw their great,
wise heads, their iron muscles bulging out their tawny
coats, their pride and power and splendor.

"Don't shoot, my brother," Fundi whispered. "Black
Mane is not here."

"Turn off the light," Albert replied.

When the moonlight crept back on the scene, the three
lions drew off a short distance. But in a moment they
remembered that this was their hour and their domain,
and that they were not fawns, but lions, so with great
dignity they returned to the feast.

The boys watched them for a full hour. Unlike the
hyenas, they did not fight over the meat, and the only
sound was the tearing of flesh from bone as they sank
their big fangs in the carcass, braced their paws against
it, and heaved back. Finally Albert's eyes began to tire
from the strain of watching. If something else did not
happen soon, he thought, he was going to get drowsy.

The thought had hardly crossed his mind, it seemed,
when he felt Fundi's elbow jab him in the ribs. Instinctively, his relaxed hands closed on his rifle and his gaze,
suddenly sharp, searched the ground. It was bare except
for the torn carcass of the zebra.

"What is it, Fundi?" he whispered.

"I don't know. The lions have run off."

"Run? Their bellies were full."

"No, they were afraid."

"What is there on this veldt to frighten Simba?" But if
there was such a thing, Albert was afraid of it too; he felt
a tightness in his throat and a chill up his back. Worse

still, Fundi was frightened, Albert could see, and of the
two, Fundi was always the second to show fear.

"Listen," Fundi whispered.

Something was approaching from downwind. A heavy,
powerful something. The brush crashed. Shrubs and saplings were being crushed down or broken off. A bold,
pugnacious something that cared not where it walked.

"Tembu?" Albert breathed. For the natives had told
him that long ago wild elephants had crossed these hills.

"I don't think so, brother. It might be buffaloes, but I
think not. Get ready, brother."

Albert sprang to his feet, so that he could shoot over
the four-foot *boma* wall. Fundi rose behind him, ready to
give him light. Thoroughly frightened—and for that reason utterly steady and still—the two boys waited.

Out of the brushwood pushed a vast shape. It was
moving straight toward the *boma*. But it was not big
enough for an elephant, too big for a buffalo, and something very like horror gripped Albert's heart as he laid
eyes on it and still did not know what it was.

Just then Fundi let go his breath in one explosive whis-
per, "Kifuru!"

Albert almost forgot the danger in a wave of wonder.
As long as he could remember he had longed for a sight
of Kifuru, and now that he had met him, it might be that
he must kill him in self-defense. The rhino had paused in
the open moonlight. His vast shape seemed too grotesque
to be alive; actually he was a holdover from Old Time.
Albert could see the two horns, one of them fully two feet
long, on his huge, nightmare head. The rhino had lowered his head, so that the horn stood out like a lance, and
he was pawing the ground. He had smelled the boys, and
ever ill-tempered and belligerent, he was about to charge.

There was no hope of dodging the animal in this four-foot cage of thorns, or of turning him with a flesh wound. Albert was taking an ugly risk not to shoot at once, for when the armored tank got its momentum, it would be hard to stop. But still his gun came reluctantly to his shoulder. The vast ungainly creature had captured his imagination as no living thing had ever done.

He signaled for Fundi to turn on the light. And then what the black boy knew as Fate, holding aloof until now, took a hand in the game.

Fundi's arm caught on the thorns of the *boma*. As the beam shot out, it focused, not on the rhino, but on a small shrub about thirty feet to one side. To behold this lowly bush suddenly light up and shine in the silvery, shadowy night somehow touched off the animal's bad temper. Snorting like a locomotive, he whirled and thundered down upon it in the full charge.

Of course, it disappeared under him. Kifuru could not understand it. He stopped, glowering about for another glimpse of his foe. And then lean little Fundi had him in the palm of his hand.

Fundi threw the flashlight beam on a ten-foot sapling, about forty feet farther on. Flinging down his head, lance pointed, Kifuru charged it. This enemy likewise disappeared in a rattle of broken twigs under his belly. Fundi next threw the light on the trunk of a stout tree, but Kifuru had had enough of such a fitful foe. His dignity outraged, he thundered off in the thorn scrub and disappeared.

Albert and Fundi laughed, but with a catch at their hearts. Two grown men could not have stood so close as they stood now, alone and together in the night. Africa was around them and in them and over them; and it was as though they knew her secrets, which only the priests of the temples of Ra had ever known, and which sometimes old safari men heard whispering. From now on, Kifuru would be for them a symbol of the untamed land they loved.

"But we may never see him again," Albert whispered.

"I think we will, my brother," Fundi answered. "You don't believe in our gods, so we'll call it luck, but Kifuru is in your fate."

Probably it was the drying up of the water holes deeper in the Blue that had brought Kifuru here, and likely the abundant fodder and shade caused him to settle down on the slopes of the hills not two miles from the mission. Yet Albert felt strangely and deeply about him, as though indeed their meeting had been fated by Fundi's gods. He had always sensed a warm kinship with the wild animals of his thorny playground, but Kifuru seemed his very own, a gift to him, more like a trust, out of Africa's wild heart.

An expert tracker, Fundi had soon found his lairs; then he and Albert visited him almost every day. Before long it was not necessary to track him. They knew his range and his feeding habits, his time for drink and time for sleep, and often they could walk straight to him, as though they heard him calling in his thorn thickets.

They followed him for hours as he browsed and spied on him as he lay asleep, like a monstrous hog, in the shade. They worshiped his great strength—it was nothing to him to break down or tear out by the roots a half-grown tree—but what delighted them most was his unfailing bad temper. He was forever in high dudgeon, always spoiling for a fight.

Every time he winded his visitors, he came snorting and puffing, ready to charge on sight, and once they had to dodge his avalanche rush down a rock-strewn hillside.

Once they saw him attack a herd of a dozen buffaloes and send them thundering off in full stampede. Twice they saw lions turn off the trail, so as not to disturb his grazing. On the other hand, he was as likely to storm at a dik-dik, two feet high.

When the Little Rains broke, Albert was afraid that Kifuru would wander back to the southern Blue, but as the year rolled on, and the Great Rains smoked all the hills, it began to appear that it would be Albert, not Kifuru, who must first go.

"I've let you wait a year longer than I should have," his father told him, "and I'm reserving a seat for you on the London plane that leaves the middle of August."

"Am I not going ahead all right with my study course?" Albert asked quietly, meeting his father's eyes. An old Afrikander now, he would rather be whipped with a *kiboko* than let the woe of his heart creep into his voice or avert his gaze.

"I must say you're making very rapid strides. But, Albert, I don't want you to grow up an old bushwhacker, more at home in a tent in the Blue than in a drawing room. I've been out here twenty years—looks as though I'll never go home, except to visit—but you. . . ."

"Where is home?" Albert's mother broke in. "For us it's Scotland, but Albert was born out here. He's an East African."

"I never expected to hear you say that, Ellen." Doctor Cruikshank glanced at his son's still face, and his own face looked troubled. "Albert, it might be arranged for you to take Fundi with you. Many young bloods from the colonies sport native servants, and he might be worth his board and keep. . . ."

Albert shook his head. "I'd rather not take Fundi, sir.

He's got to have the sun. He's part of all this." Albert's
gaze roamed to the window.

"Then he'll have to wait for your return. The middle of
August, Albert."

With his head up, Albert walked out of the room. It
was not only leaving Fundi and Kifuru but losing Africa.
He would never regain it. This was his dark premonition.
After four years, the trail he had followed would be cold.
He would be another alien in the colony, a visiting
Scotchman who made an occasional safari into the Blue.

He and Kifuru need never have met, he brooded. Yet
before the gods of the sun and moon brought the day for
his departure, it was given him to fight for Kifuru's life.

Kanano, the Cruikshanks' cook, gave the first news of
the trouble, when he came to work on an early August
morning. On the preceding evening, he said, three lorries
had rolled up the long road from Nairobi and had
stopped at Mamba Springs, three miles from the mission.
It was big safari, with many guns, countless camp boys
and two great *bwanas*. From the description, Albert recognized one *bwana* as Frank Lewis, a white guide. The
other was undoubtedly a millionaire sportsman from
across the sea.

At first, Albert was not greatly alarmed. Safaris heading southward frequently stopped for the night at
Mamba Springs. But Kanano said the tents had been
strongly pitched. One of the gunbearers had told him
that the *bwanas* were looking for rhino.

"Rhino?" Albert breathed.

"They have word of a very large rhino, with a horn
worth a thousand rupees, in an hour's walk from Mamba
Springs."

Albert went to his room and got his heavy rifle. Then he sped to Fundi's hut and called him softly. But when he had revealed the situation in less than a score of words, he did not know what to do next. To attempt to stampede Kifuru from his lair might result only in driving him to the alien guns.

"We'll go to this camp, my brother, and see what is to be seen," Fundi said. "Perhaps we can draw a zebra across Kifuru's trail."

So they borrowed the doctor's lorry, and in ten minutes were gazing, narrow eyed, at the safari. Kanano had not exaggerated its size and opulence. Frank Lewis and his charge, a stockily built, ruddy-cheeked, pleasant-looking man about fifty years old, were eating breakfast at a folding camp table, served by a Swahili boy. Albert approached them without a sign on his lean, tanned face. Fundi hung back, as was fitting.

"You're just the fellow we want to see," Frank Lewis told his guest. "Meet Mr. Warner, from the States. Mr. Warner, Albert Cruikshank, the son of the medical missionary over on the hill."

Albert had never met a more close and studious gaze. This man would not be easy to take wild-goose chasing. Yet it was a friendly gaze, the eyes lighting up instead of filming over.

"Well," the American said, "are you the kind of chap they raise out here?"

"Look, Albert," Lewis broke in. "Mr. Warner wants an old male rhino for a museum group. We've camped a couple of days with the hope of picking up that big fellow that hangs out around here."

"Are you sure he's still in the country?" Albert parried.

"Positive. He used the water hole at the foot of Tui Kilama less than a week ago."

"Still, it's a needle in a haystack. Wouldn't it be better to go on into the Blue. . . ."

"But Mr. Warner has his blood up for this special rhino. It appears that he's a specimen in a hundred. I'm going to spend today scouting east of Tui Kilama. I thought I'd send Mr. Warner out with one of the gun-bearers to look along the western side. If we don't find him, tomorrow we'll look farther south. If you, or that boy of yours, have any suggestions. . . ."

Albert's thoughts ran in a cold, swift stream. Lewis would not find Kifuru east of Tui Kalama. Nor could he be found farther south, on tomorrow's hunt. His only real danger was today, when Mr. Warner sought him on the western side. Albert and Fundi had seen him there no later than yesterday morning. A very real danger, judging by Mr. Warner's steady hands and intent eyes.

"Instead of sending him out with a gunbearer, why not let him go with Fundi and me?" Albert asked calmly.

Lewis hesitated, but Mr. Warner said quickly, "Suits me from the ground up."

"We know every foot of that area," Albert went on, "and we'd have every chance of finding him, if he's there."

"Anyway, we'll have a big time," Mr. Warner turned, his face lighting, to Albert. "When do we start?"

They started as soon as Mr. Warner finished breakfast and got his gun. In the meantime, it was not necessary for Albert to confide his plan to Fundi. They could tell each other more in one glance than most friends could reveal in an exchange of letters; and when they stood close, just the knuckles of their hands touching, in the wonderful radiant dawn when the veldt spread and spread, or in the hushed, haunted twilight when the great beasts came forth, then their thoughts seemed to move in one stream, its every eddy and ripple known to them both. But Kifuru's life was at stake today, so a few furtive words passed between them.

The plan was simply to prevent Warner from getting sight or sound of Kifuru, or crossing his trail, warm or cold.

They left the lorry when the rocks began. Before they had covered half a mile, Albert realized that he was guiding one of the keenest hunters he had ever met. More than a hunter, he was a naturalist, an outdoor man of the highest type. Except for the risk to Kifuru and the harrowing strain of keeping him at a distance, this would have been one of the happiest mornings in Albert's life. Mr. Warner liked every dik-dik that bounded across his path, heard the call of the birds, wanted to know the meanings of all signs, and never raised his gun.

Usually rather quiet with strangers, Albert felt himself impelled to talk. He explained why the black leopards, born in the same litter with common spotted ones, were the more fierce and dangerous. He gave his reasons why the giraffes had so little to fear from lions. Before long he was talking about Kifuru too. His glowing descriptions seemed to flow from his tongue unawares.

"I've got a daughter about your age," Mr. Warner told him, "waiting with her mother in Nairobi. I wish she were with us, to see and hear all this."

Presently they saw a small herd of eland, led by a big, sleek bull with magnificent spiraled horns. It occurred to Albert that if Mr. Warner would shoot the bull, he might be diverted from his main objective. Albert admired the

fine beast, but his life would be a cheap price to pay for
Kifuru's safety.

"I doubt if you'll see a finer eland on your trip," he told
Mr. Warner.

"But I don't want an eland." And then Warner turned
and gazed, with a puzzled expression, into his young
guide's face.

Albert led him across a dry watercourse and on to a
thorn-grown plateau where he had never known Kifuru
to come. From here he intended to make a big circle
through lion country, back to the lorry. But the gods
hated him, he thought. They were not content to drive
him from the country, but must stab him in the back
before he went. Walking at the rear of the file of three,
Fundi took a little stick and broke it in his hand.

Albert heard it crack. It was not a prearranged signal,
but knowing Fundi he knew there was danger here. In-
stantly, he turned toward the naked ground on his left,
praying that Warner would follow blindly. But as he
wheeled, out of the corner of his eye he saw what looked
like a big, dark anthill in the middle of a thorn thicket
about a hundred yards to his right.

There was still hope. Warner's eyes were new to
Africa. The wind was treacherous on this plateau, but its
general flow would carry the man smell some distance
forward of Kifuru's bed. But a crosscurrent flung the
taint of it into his sensitive nostrils. He hated it with all
his two-ton capacity for hatred. With a snort that shattered the silence of this thorny waste, he sprang to his
feet.

Warner saw him and ran forward, as though for a
clearer view. Many rhinos, almost all except the most
stupid or the worst tempered, would have seized the

chance to bolt, but not Kifuru. Snorting and stamping, he advanced to the edge of the thicket. Never before had Albert seen him so defiant, so great. It was the most glorious wilderness picture he had ever beheld.

But there was nothing he could do to preserve it. To put a flesh wound in Kifuru's side would only make him charge. Yet he did not look away. He was compelled, he did not know why, to gaze with supreme intensity, in spite of the horror in his heart of Warner's up-leaping gun. He must see and interpret every movement, clear and fast as lightning.

He heard both barrels roar. Still Kifuru did not fall, did not run; instead he advanced a dozen angry paces. Albert could hardly believe that Warner had missed the huge target at such close range, but there was not the slightest sign of a hit. And now Warner had opened the breech of his gun to insert two fresh cartridges. He started to shut the breech. . . .

The rest was long and drawn and remote, like events in a bad dream. Warner seemed to have difficulty closing the lock of his rifle. His movements became hurried, then frantic. He was trying to force the gun closed. He was exerting terrific power. Meanwhile Kifuru had lowered his point. He was moving forward. He was trotting. Now, with a great snort, he launched into the charge.

He had perhaps forty yards to go. He would run blind, Albert knew, and Warner could swing aside and dodge him if he were alert and agile enough, but instead he still worked desperately with his disabled gun. The distance narrowed. A fast horse could hardly outrun Kifuru in a short race. His fore and hind quarters pumped up and down, alternatively, in that clumsy but terrifying rhino gallop. His horn was a lance in rest.

Albert had never seen him so magnificent. He would never forget this last great charge of Kifuru. But even as the picture was burning into his memory, his big double rifle was leaping to his shoulder. He glanced quickly along the sights. He squeezed the trigger.

There was not a sound as he walked to the dead rhino and gazed down at him. Warner came up quietly and stood beside him, but he did not look at the fallen; instead he gazed with wide, wondering eyes into Albert's face.

Finally he spoke, "I'm sorry, son."

"It couldn't be helped."

"I want you to know something. I fired those two bullets in the air, trying to scare him off. I should have guessed before, but I didn't—about you and the rhino, I mean. It dawned on me only when I saw him. He was something to see, wasn't he?"

"I tell you!"

"Others can see him now, at least get an idea of him, in our museum. People who will never get a chance to know all this." Warner made a comprehensive gesture with his hand. "That's something, isn't it?"

"Yes. Quite a lot."

"And lives are bought with lives. That seems to be the law. You know it, too, Albert. You were willing to have me shoot the eland to save your rhino. But you had to kill your rhino to save me."

"I tried to lead you away from him. You know that?"

"I got it, son, finally. But maybe it's all for the best. You won't believe that now, but later, perhaps, you'll see. I'm going to have a talk with your father."

"I don't understand." For the reaction was setting in, and Albert felt dazed.

"This is just a preliminary trip. In two weeks I'm returning to Nairobi to assemble my outfit for six months in the Blue. I'm going there partly to get some specimens for our museum, mostly to find out about Africa. But we'll go into the details later, with your dad."

THE
MYSTERY
OF
KEESH
Jack London

■

■■■
Keesh lived long ago on the rim of the polar sea, was headman of his village through many and prosperous years, and died full of honors with his name on the lips of men. So long ago did he live that only the old men remember his name, his name and the tale, which they got from the old men before them, and which the old men to come will tell to their children and their children's children down to the end of time. And the winter darkness, when the north gales make their long sweep across the icepack and the air is filled with flying white and no man may venture forth, is the chosen time for the telling of how Keesh, from the poorest igloo in the village, rose to power and place over them all.

He was a bright boy, so the tale runs, healthy and strong, and he had seen thirteen suns, in their way of reckoning time. For each winter the sun leaves the land in darkness, and the next year a new sun returns so that they may be warm again and look upon one another's faces. The father of Keesh had been a very brave man, but he had met his death in a time of famine, when he sought to save the lives of his people by taking the life of a great polar bear. In his eagerness he came to close grapples with the bear, and his bones were crushed; but the bear had much meat on him and the people were saved. Keesh was his only son, and afterward Keesh lived alone with his mother. But the people are prone to forget, and they forgot the deed of his father; and he being but a boy and his mother only a woman, they too were swiftly forgotten, and before long came to live in the meanest of all the igloos.

It was at a council one night in the big igloo of Klosh-Kwan, the chief, that Keesh showed the blood that ran in his veins and the manhood that stiffened his back. With the dignity of an elder, he rose to his feet, and waited for silence amid the babble of voices.

"It is true that meat be apportioned me and mine," he said. "But it is ofttimes old and tough, this meat, and moreover it has an unusual quantity of bones."

The hunters, grizzled and gray, and lusty and young, were aghast. The like had never been known before. A child, that talked like a grown man and said harsh things to their very faces!

But steadily and with seriousness, Keesh went on. "For that I know my father, Bok, was a great hunter, I speak these words. It is said that Bok brought home more meat than any of the two best hunters, that with his own hands he attended to the division of it, that with his own eyes he saw to it that the least old woman and the last old man received fair share."

"Na! Na!" the men cried. "Put the child out!" "Send him off to bed!" "He is no man that he should talk to men and graybeards!"

He waited calmly till the uproar died down.

"Thou hast a wife, Ugh-Gluk," he said, "and for her dost thou speak. And thou, too, Massuk, a mother also, and for them dost thou speak. My mother has no one, save me; wherefore I speak. As I say, though Bok be dead because he hunted over keenly, it is just that I, who am his son, and that Ikeega, who is my mother and was his wife, should have meat in plenty so long as there be meat in plenty in the tribe. I, Keesh, the son of Bok, have spoken."

He sat down, his ears keenly alert to the flood of protest and indignation his words had created.

"That a boy should speak in council!" old Ugh-Gluk was mumbling.

"Shall the babes in arms tell us men the things we shall do?" Massuk demanded in a loud voice. "Am I a man that I should be made a mock by every child that cries for meat?"

The anger boiled to a white heat. They ordered him to bed, threatened that he should have no meat at all, and promised him sore beatings for his presumption. Keesh's eyes began to flash, and the blood to pound darkly under his skin. In the midst of the abuse he sprang to his feet.

"Hear me, ye men!" he cried. "Never shall I speak in the council again, never again till the men come to me and say, 'It is well, Keesh, that thou shouldst speak, it is well and it is our wish.' Take this now, ye men, for my last word. Bok, my father, was a great hunter. I, too, his son, shall go and hunt the meat that I eat. And be it known, now, that the division of that which I kill shall be fair. And no widow nor weak one shall cry in the night because there is no meat, when the strong men are groaning in great pain for that they have eaten overmuch. And in the days to come there shall be shame upon the strong men who have eaten overmuch. I, Keesh, have said it!"

Jeers and scornful laughter followed him out of the igloo, but his jaw was set and he went his way, looking neither to right nor left.

The next day he went forth along the shoreline where the ice and the land met together. Those who saw him go noted that he carried his bow, with a goodly supply of bone-barbed arrows, and that across his shoulder was his father's big hunting spear. And there was laughter, and much talk, at the event. It was an unprecedented occurrence. Never did boys of his tender age go forth to hunt, much less to hunt alone. Also were there shaking of heads and prophetic mutterings, and the women looked pityingly at Ikeega, and her face was grave and sad.

"He will be back ere long," they said cheerin

"Let him go; it will teach him a lesson," th
said. "And he will come back shortly, and he will b
meek and soft of speech in the days to follow."

But a day passed, and a second, and on the third a wild
gale blew, and there was no Keesh. Ikeega tore her hair
and put soot of the seal oil on her face in token of her
grief; and the women assailed the men with bitter words
in that they had mistreated the boy and sent him to his
death; and the men made no answer, preparing to go in
search of the body when the storm abated.

Early next morning, however, Keesh strode into the
village. But he came not shamefacedly. Across his shoulders he bore a burden of fresh-killed meat. And there was
importance in his step and arrogance in his speech.

"Go, ye men, with the dogs and sleds, and take my
trail for the better part of a day's travel," he said. "There
is much meat on the ice—a she-bear and two half-grown
cubs."

Ikeega was overcome with joy, but he received her
demonstrations in manlike fashion, saying, "Come,
Ikeega, let us eat. And after that I shall sleep, for I am
weary."

And he passed into their igloo and ate profoundly, and
afterward slept for twenty running hours.

There was much doubt at first, much doubt and dis-
cussion. The killing of a polar bear is very dangerous,
and thrice dangerous is it, and three times thrice, to kill a
mother bear with her cubs. The men could not bring
themselves to believe that the boy Keesh, singlehanded,
had accomplished so great a marvel. But the women
spoke of the fresh-killed meat he had brought on his
back, and this was an overwhelming argument against
their unbelief. So they finally departed, grumbling

greatly that in all probability, if the thing were so, he had neglected to cut up the carcasses.

Now in the north it is very necessary that this should be done as soon as a kill is made. If not, the meat freezes so soldily as to turn the edge of the sharpest knife, and a 300-pound bear, frozen stiff, is no easy thing to put upon a sled and haul over the rough ice. But arrived at the spot, they found not only the kill, which they had doubted, but that Keesh had quartered the beasts in true hunter fashion, and removed the entrails.

Thus began the mystery of Keesh, a mystery that deepened and deepened with the passing of the days. His very next trip he killed a young bear, nearly full-grown, and on the trip following, a large male bear and his mate. He was ordinarily gone from three to four days, though it was nothing unusual for him to stay away a week at a time on the ice field. Always he declined company on these expeditions, and the people marveled.

"How does he do it?" they demanded of one another. "Never does he take a dog with him, and dogs are of such great help, too."

"Why dost thou hunt only bear?" Klosh-Kwan once ventured to ask him.

And Keesh made fitting answer. "It is well known that there is more meat on the bear," he said.

But there was also talk of witchcraft in the village. "He hunts with evil spirits," some of the people contended, "wherefore his hunting is rewarded. How else can it be, save that he hunts with evil spirits?"

"Mayhap they be not evil, but good, these spirits," others said. "It is known that his father was a mighty hunter. May not his father hunt with him so that he may attain excellence and patience and understanding? Who knows?"

Nonetheless his success continued, and the less skillful hunters were often kept busy hauling in his meat. And in the division of it he was just. As his father had done before him, he saw to it that the least old woman and the last old man received a fair portion, keeping no more for himself than his needs required. And because of this, and of his merit as a hunter, he was looked upon with respect and even awe, and there was talk of making him chief after old Klosh-Kwan. Because of the things he had done, they looked for him to appear again in the council, but he never came, and they were ashamed to ask.

"I am minded to build me an igloo," he said one day to Klosh-Kwan and a number of the hunters. "It shall be a large igloo, wherein Ikeega and I can dwell in comfort."

"Ay." They nodded gravely.

"But I have no time. My business is hunting, and it takes all my time. So it is but just that the men and women who eat my meat should build me my igloo."

And the igloo was built accordingly, on a generous scale which exceeded even the dwelling of Klosh-Kwan. Keesh and his mother moved into it, and it was the first prosperity she had enjoyed since the death of Bok. Nor was material prosperity alone hers, for, because of her wonderful son and the position he had given her, she came to be looked upon as the first woman in all the village; the women were given to visiting her, to asking her advice, and to quoting her wisdom when arguments arose among themselves or with the men.

But it was the mystery of Keesh's marvelous hunting that took chief place in all their minds. And one day Ugh-Gluk taxed him with witchcraft to his face.

"It is charged," Ugh-Gluk said ominously, "that thou dealest with evil spirits, wherefore thy hunting is rewarded."

"Is not the meat good?" Keesh made answer. "Has one in the village yet to fall sick from eating of it? How dost thou know that witchcraft be concerned? Or dost thou guess, in the dark, merely because of the envy that consumes thee?"

And Ugh-Gluk withdrew discomfited, the women laughing at him as he walked away. But in the council one night, after long deliberation, it was determined to put spies on his track when he went forth to hunt, so that his methods might be learned. So on his next trip, Bim and Bawn, two young men, and the craftiest of hunters, followed after him, taking care not to be seen. After five days they returned, their eyes bulging and their tongues a-tremble to tell what they had seen. The council was hastily called in Klosh-Kwan's dwelling, and Bim took up the tale.

"Brothers! As commanded, we journeyed on the trail of Keesh, and cunningly we journeyed, so that he might not know. And midway of the first day he picked up with a great he-bear. It was a very great bear."

"None greater," Bawn corroborated, and went on himself. "Yet was the bear not inclined to fight, for he turned away and made off slowly over the ice. This we saw from the rocks of the shore, and the bear came toward us, and after him came Keesh, very much unafraid. And he shouted harsh words after the bear and waved his arms about and made much noise. Then did the bear grow angry and rise up on his hind legs and growl. But Keesh walked right up to the bear."

"Ay," Bim continued the story. "Right up to the bear Keesh walked. And the bear took after him, and Keesh ran away. But as he ran he dropped a little round ball on the ice. And the bear stopped and smelled of it, then swallowed it up. And Keesh continued to run away and drop little round balls, and the bear continued to swallow them up."

Exclamations and cries of doubt were being made, and Ugh-Gluk expressed open unbelief.

"With our own eyes we saw it," Bim affirmed.

And Bawn: "Ay, with our own eyes. And this continued until the bear stood suddenly upright and cried aloud in pain and thrashed his forepaws madly about. And Keesh continued to make off over the ice to safe distance. But the bear gave him no notice, being occupied with the misfortune the little round balls had wrought within him."

"Ay, within him," Bim interrupted. "For he did claw at himself and leap about over the ice like a playful puppy, save from the way he growled and squealed it was plain it was not play but pain. Never did I see such a sight!"

"Nay, never was such a sight seen," Bawn took up the strain. "And, furthermore, it was such a large bear."

"Witchcraft," Ugh-Gluk suggested.

"I know not," Bawn replied. "I tell only of what my eyes beheld. And after a while the bear grew weak and tired, for he was very heavy and he had jumped about with exceeding violence, and he went off along the shore ice, shaking his head slowly from side to side and sitting down ever and again to squeal and cry. And Keesh followed after the bear, and we followed after Keesh, and for that day and three days more we followed. The bear grew weak and never ceased crying from his pain."

"It was a charm!" Ugh-Gluk exclaimed. "Surely it was a charm!"

"It may well be."

And Bim relieved Bawn. "The bear wandered, now this way and now that, doubling back and forth and crossing his trail in circles, so that at the end he was near where

Keesh had first come upon him. By this time he was quite sick, the bear, and could crawl no farther, so Keesh came up close and speared him to death."

"And then?" Klosh-Kwan demanded.

"Then we left Keesh skinning the bear and came running that the news of the killing might be told."

And in the afternoon of that day the women hauled in the meat of the bear while the men sat in council assembled. When Keesh arrived a messenger was sent to him, bidding him to come to the council. But he sent reply, saying that he was hungry and tired, also that his igloo was large and comfortable and could hold many men.

And curiosity was so strong on the men that the whole council, Klosh-Kwan to the fore, rose up and went to the igloo of Keesh. He was eating, but he received them with respect and seated them according to their rank. Ikeega was proud and embarrassed by turns, but Keesh was quite composed.

Klosh-Kwan recited the information brought by Bim and Bawn, and at its close said in a stern voice, "So explanation is wanted, O Keesh, of thy manner of hunting. Is there witchcraft in it?"

Keesh looked up and smiled. "Nay, O Klosh-Kwan. It is not for a boy to know aught of witches, and of witches I know nothing. I have but devised a means whereby I may kill the ice bear with ease, that is all. It be head craft, not witchcraft."

"And may any man?"

"Any man."

There was a long silence. The men looked in one another's faces, and Keesh went on eating.

"And ... and ... and wilt thou tell us, O Keesh?" Klosh-Kwan finally asked in a tremulous voice.

"Yea, I will tell thee." Keesh finished sucking a marrowbone and rose to his feet. "It is quite simple. Behold!"

Keesh picked up a thin strip of whalebone and showed it to them. The ends were sharp as needlepoints. The strip he coiled carefully, till it disappeared in his hand. Then, as he suddenly released it, it sprang straight again. He picked up a piece of blubber.

"So," he said, "one takes a small chunk of blubber, thus, and thus makes it hollow. Then into the hollow goes the whalebone, so, tightly coiled, and another piece of blubber is fitted over the whalebone. After that it is put outside where it freezes into a little round ball. The bear swallows the little round ball, the blubber melts, the whalebone with its sharp ends stands out straight, the bear gets sick, and when the bear is very sick, why, you kill him with a spear. It is quite simple."

And Ugh-Gluk said "Oh!" and Klosh-Kwan said "Ah!" And each said something after his own manner, and all understood.

And this is the story of Keesh, who lived long ago on the rim of the polar sea. Because he exercised head craft and not witchcraft, he rose from the meanest igloo to be headman of his village, and through all the years that he lived, it is related, his tribe was prosperous, and neither widow nor weak one cried aloud in the night because there was no meat.

A
MASTER
FOR
PSALMSINGER
Dion Henderson

■

■■■

My old man came out on the veranda and smoked his pipe after supper, watching me pull the leather bird for the big lemon-and-white pointer dog we called Psalmsinger. A leather bird is what you use to help pointer puppies in training, to make them steady on point. It's just a roll of leather stuffed with rags and with some feathers tied onto it; you drag it on a fish pole at the end of a long line, so the puppies don't know you're doing it. When you drag it through the grass they chase it, and when you stop you holler, "Whoa"; and pretty quick they will point it, like they had found a real bird and had made it hold still for them. But when you do it with a trained dog like Psalmsinger you're just fooling around. But the dog knew it too, so it didn't hurt anything.

"I know how you can get to college," my old man said presently. "You can sell that dog to Jonathan."

That was sort of a joke.

Jonathan was a friend of my old man's from their days in the city. Jonathan had kept making money so that someday he could do all the hunting and fishing he wanted, while my old man had kept losing what money he had, from doing his hunting and fishing right then. About the time we were out of money and came back to live at the old place with the dogs where the hunting and fishing didn't cost anything, Jonathan had saved up enough to do what he wanted. But somehow Jonathan never quite made a success of it.

"There's different kinds of success," my old man said. "A man who makes a success out of working when his friends are playing may have a little trouble learning how to play when his friends are played out."

Probably that makes some kind of sense, when you're old enough to figure it out. Anyway, Jonathan kept coming out to our place for some hunting and fishing, but mostly to talk to my old man about what he should do next. And to look at the dogs. More than anything else, I guess Jonathan wanted to own a real top hunting dog. At first my old man gave him advice and went over pedigrees with him, and Jonathan bought two or three promising young dogs. One at a time, that is. But somehow they didn't work out for him, and Jonathan felt bad about it and found good homes for them.

"Don't blame yourself too much," my old man told him. "They were youngsters, just derbies or a little better, and a lot of things can go wrong with a bird dog. After all, you know the saying."

I don't know whether Jonathan knew the saying or not. But I did, and it's a thing to remember if you ever have a mind to buy yourself a top dog: the only way to buy the best is to be first man at the funeral of the feller that owned him.

There's also something about having to take the widow in the bargain, but I forget how that goes.

It was when Jonathan's dogs didn't work out for him that he started mooning around our dogs; that was when the joke got started. It was a very private joke, between me and my old man. If Jonathan had known about it his feelings might have been hurt, and neither me nor my old man would have hurt his feelings for anything. But my old man sold him one of our class dogs—a big winning dog too—and about two months later the dog ran away from Jonathan up in Canada and showed up at home nearly a year later. The dog was all right, except that it was skinny, until Jonathan came around; and then the dog chased Jonathan all the way down around the lake and up a tree on the other side. My old man gave Jonathan his money back—he was very strict about things like that.

After a time, Jonathan wanted another dog, and he took on so wistful about it that my old man took his money again. But this time he just put it aside, and when Jonathan brought the dog home my old man took the money out of the sideboard and gave it to him and never cracked a smile.

Now, sitting on the veranda watching me fool with Psalmsinger, my old man said, grinning, "Sure, sell him to Jonathan. You'll be lucky if it pays your way through the eighth grade."

"I get out of the eighth grade next spring," I told him, being a little cool about it.

"That's what I mean, boy," my old man said.

There still was time to play with the leather bird once more before dark, and so I made Psalmsinger hup over on one end of the lawn—that was enough in itself to give my old man goose bumps, making a pointer hup like a spaniel—and I went on down across the lawn to where the tall grass started. There was a car coming up the long drive between the spruce, but I was busy. I took the leather bird and threw it out as far as the line would go and then I waved Psalmsinger forward. He made the turf-digging drive of a field-trial dog and cast into the field fifty yards just for the fun of running. Then, still running with that effortless drive, he came upwind toward where the leather bird was in the grass; and suddenly, not slowing but stopping all at once, he changed from a white-and-lemon streak to a statue, like that: point!

"The psalm-singing son of a gun," my old man said softly from the steps. He said it partly in admiration and partly in disgust, because of the secret we three had, the secret that made the dog eligible for a boy to fool around with, instead of being an untouchable aristocrat back in the kennels. The dog held there, so staunch you thought maybe he had died and turned to stone, so still that maybe he was not a dog at all, but stone to begin with, and you only imagined that he had run in the way that light moves.

My old man said it again, what he said before. That was how Psalmsinger got his name. My old man kept calling him that, after we found out about him, and so we registered him that way.

The car I had heard on the drive had stopped behind the house somewhere, and I could see someone else was on the porch now with my old man. That was all right with me. I wasn't above a little showing off for company.

I flipped the fish pole hard and the leather bird came out of the grass a yard from Psalmsinger's nose, but he didn't even blink. It went flopping through the air like a quail tipped over in flight and fell into the grass again thirty feet away, but Psalmsinger didn't move at all, except that the little flaps on his nostrils flared. Then I waved my hand to him, and he broke the point and followed, not charging hard now, but quickly and softly, and I pulled the bird a little farther, in short jerks, and he drew lower and lower, stepping with a quick, precise, ballet-dancer's step. And then I left the bird, and Psalmsinger was on point again. His tail was lifted high but his head remained low, and he stood with the intensity you need on relocation of a skittish bird.

That's the way it was. Make-believe or not, it was the kind of dog work that would raise the hair on any bird hunter's head. I clapped my hands and said, "All right," and Psalmsinger relaxed and pranced over to me, and you could see he knew very well that it was just fooling around and wouldn't hurt anything.

Afterward we walked up to the veranda, and I saw it was Jonathan there, talking excitedly to my old man.

"His name is Psalmsinger," my old man was saying. "He is down from Lady Ferris and the Proctor dog and bred as high as any pointer you'll ever see. His manners are excellent, his style flawless, and he isn't for sale. That's all you need to know about him, Jonathan."

And then, before I even got onto the veranda to say hello to Jonathan, my old man said, "Take the dog back to the kennels."

I opened my mouth to object, because Psalmsinger wasn't in the kennel one night out of three, but there was a certain tone in my old man's voice. "Yes, sir," I said. I'd brag about him some other time.

But Jonathan came down off the steps, and said, "Boy."

He didn't mean me. He looked at the dog and the dog looked at him. He held out his hand, knuckles up, the way you do to a trial dog if you have good sense, and Psalmsinger sniffed politely and then his tail wagged a little.

I was astonished. I never saw Psalmsinger wag his tail to anyone, except sometimes when he was happy about working. But usually he wasn't happy about working—not his real work—so he didn't get very much chance to wag his tail.

"Say," I said to the old man. "Did you see that?"

"Take him to the kennel," my old man said flatly. "Take him now."

It was our secret that he was protecting now.

Jonathan said, "What's the matter with him?"

My old man said, "You just saw him work, there with the leather bird. He's always that good, sometimes he's even better. He's a good dog."

He was, too. He was always stylish and frequently really artistic and occasionally even memorable. But it was all make-believe. It was make-believe whether we worked with birds or the dummy leather and feathers. And when the guns came out and spoke to the rising covey in the fields, and it no longer was make-believe, then it was nothing. That was our secret.

In the beginning, of course, we didn't know how it would be. Psalmsinger was one of the dogs my old man had planned for, two or three generations of planning, and the pick of the final litter. My old man thought very highly of him, even before he was born. And when he was a puppy, he looked to be worth it all. He was tall and handsome, standing over good ground and with a lot of daylight under him, the way the best dogs ought to be nowadays. And he never had the awkwardness most puppies have learning to run. He was born to run and he loved it, in his quiet way. The other love he had was the birds, the quail. That was quiet too, and intense, but there was no way to tell that the quiet and intense love that gave the pup so much promise would make him useless at the work he was bred and born to.

My old man started him in a few puppy trials, because that is part of the responsibility you have to a dog, to let him become as good as he wants to, even though that means sometimes he becomes too good to be your dog anymore. Mostly that is not much of a risk, but it was with Psalmsinger. While he was still eligible for the puppy stakes—that's fourteen months—my old man could have sold him for enough to put a new roof on the old place. But we still have the old one.

Anyhow, Psalmsinger loved the birds and that was fine, and if it hadn't been for the hunting no one would have known his secret. But around our place the dogs have to hunt. To hunt is the real beginning for them; where they go from there is up to them and the way my old man feels, but the honest hunting is where they start.

The first time Psalmsinger was braced with High Design. He went out wide across a cornfield and into stubble and on to where a ridge bent him; High Design looked after him once with the cold look she has for the young dogs, and afterward she didn't look at him. She is a veteran dog who has seen the young ones come and go, and to her they are just different skins full of the same dogs going wide beyond her, and when the day is over she doesn't recognize them and neither does my old man. But sometimes at the end of the day she acts as though she knows them after all, and then my old man pays attention, because High Design is one of the dogs you measure other dogs with.

A high hour after she and Psalmsinger went out together he ceased to exist as far as she was concerned, and my old man had that expression, part admiration and part disgust, on his face. Then it happened. Psalmsinger found a small covey and handled it beautifully, even though he flagged a little at the pleasure of having the bird smell in his nose. High Design came up to honor his point, and you could tell from the way she moved that possibly she would recognize this dog. Then the birds came out and my old man dropped one for him with the little gun.

Psalmsinger stood, very steady at shot, and the quail pinwheeled out in a little puff of feathers and hit the stubble with a thump, and my old man said happily, "Fetch."

Psalmsinger stood still and my old man spoke to him again. Then Psalmsinger went forward with a strange uneasy gait and nosed the bird and turned it over and looked at my old man with a strange, sorry expression. Then he nosed the bird again, but it was dead all right. Then he turned his muzzle upward and howled, an unmistakable lament for the death of a beloved bird.

My old man sat down suddenly in the field and looked at Psalmsinger and the dog looked back at him, tall and beautiful but sorry, sorry that a bird had been killed. He was a dog in whom the cherished love of game birds had somehow got out of hand, a dog bred so finely to a kind of hunting that is half an art form anyway that he couldn't bear the scent of blood and death.

"He never saw a bird killed before," my old man said, not angry as I'd seen him angry when a dog went sour, in fact not angry at all. "He learned to fetch with the dummies, and he trained with birds that were not hurt, and he ran in the trials where there was only the token pistol shot."

I stood there, partly expecting my old man to get up regretfully and shoot Psalmsinger, and I guess the expectation showed on my face.

"Don't be so grim," my old man said. "This isn't the dog's fault. He didn't order the heart that's in him, any more than he arranged his bones and the color of his hide."

And then I knew what he meant when he said if you wanted to take the credit for the dogs you bred, you had to take the blame, and most dog breeders would come off better if they'd decline both.

So we went home and that was that, except that my old man never took Psalmsinger anywhere again, and he let me do whatever I wanted with the dog. He said Psalmsinger was my dog, but it was only a formal arrangement because the dog and I were sort of associates in a very exclusive company. Neither one of us was allowed to have anything to do with the really important dogs or the trials or the hunting trips. As it turned out, Psalmsinger was very good with the puppies who had to learn how to run, and he picked up young birds that fell out of nests and brought them tenderly home, so that I had pet robins and crows and blackbirds and goodness knows what.

Sometimes my old man got sort of fussed at us, and said, "I'm in great shape around here. The two most promising critters on the place are a kid who figures college is where good folks go when they die, and a dog who figures he's kinfolk to the dickeybirds."

"He don't either," I said. "He likes all birds, but it's just the quail he loves."

"Doesn't either," my old man said, correcting me. "You've a long ways to go before you get to college."

He was spoofing me a little then, but it was all right. Maybe I started worrying about college a little early, but it seemed to me that going to college cost a lot more than we were likely to have unless we spent quite a while getting it together.

Then there was the time Jonathan came and saw me fooling around with Psalmsinger and the leather bird. He had a new gun to show my old man, a lovely handmade shotgun with the stock built up especially to fit him, and a grooved forearm, and all the gold and silver set in the receiver making patterns of birds and dogs.

"Will it help on those passing shots?" my old man asked him, grinning.

"Which one you thinking of?" Jonathan demanded, grinning too.

My old man always said Jonathan was a lousy shot. But my old man was such a beautiful, offhand, casual, deadly wing shot that he said that about most other men. But he wasn't fooling about Jonathan.

"Well," my old man said, "I was thinking of the time last fall you got up on the knoll and the quail flew right around it two or three times."

"And I had a chance to reload twice and missed him all six times," Jonathan said happily. "I remember."

He didn't worry about his shooting. He loved it, just doing it, and being able to do it, whenever he wanted, no matter what the cost.

After they were through talking about the new gun, Jonathan wanted to see Psalmsinger again, but my old man talked him out of it. The next week he came back, and my old man let him talk to Psalmsinger in the kennel, but that was all.

Afterward I asked my old man why he was so set on what he wouldn't do, and he looked at me with one eyebrow kind of cocked. "You're going on twelve now, boy?"

"Yes, sir," I said.

"Fixing to go to college, another four or five years?"

"Five," I said.

"Then I'll tell you a thing that may help you along the way," my old man said. "This is mostly about dogs, but you may have some kids of your own someday—who want to know about dogs, that is," he said. "It's a proper thing to subdue the wild streaks, and to bend the strong wills so long as you don't break them. Yes, and to teach manners to the ones who don't reckon they'll be mannerly."

"Yes, sir," I said.

"But you don't change the heart in them, which is something you don't know about, and make it into something you do. No, you let the heart in them be the way it has to be, and either you get along with them or you get along without them."

"Yes, sir," I said.

"Talking about dogs, you know," my old man said.

"Yes, sir," I said. "But I might have some kids of my own someday."

"Who want to know about dogs," he prompted.

"Yes, sir," I said.

"One more thing," my old man said. "When there's a heart in them you don't understand, you keep it to yourself. You don't laugh at it. And you don't let anyone else laugh at it."

"Yes, sir," I said. "Now I understand."

"I doubt it," my old man said. "But wait until you get to college and study up a little."

Just the same, I think I understood pretty well. My old man didn't go around talking like that every day. He gave me a good chance to think about what he said betweentimes.

That summer Jonathan came up several more times, on one excuse or another, but what he really came for was to see the dog. I could see my old man getting troubled, because the dog reacted to Jonathan like nothing my old man had ever seen before, and Jonathan was the same way.

"Look what happened to the good dogs he had," my old man said. "I don't know what he did, or how, but look what happened. Some of them dogs never did get over spending a few months with him."

It didn't look like the time for me to say anything.

"Can you imagine what would happen, you get Psalm-singer with a shooting fool like Jonathan?"

"No, sir," I said.

"Neither can I," my old man said. "I'm afraid I couldn't bear to find out."

That wasn't the time for me to speak up either.

But the next time Jonathan came, my old man wasn't home. Psalmsinger was out in the yard, and when Jona-than got out of his car Psalmsinger went bouncing over like a puppy, tail wagging. It like to broke me up.

Jonathan came over and sat on the steps beside me, with Psalmsinger sitting in front of him, head cocked and waiting. "Why won't your pop sell me this dog?"

"He's my dog," I said.

"Well, why won't you sell him to me?" Jonathan asked.

"Because my old man ain't overjoyed with the way you got along with the other ones."

"What's the matter with this one?"

"He's a good dog," I said. "He's a dog with a heart as big as a tiger. But different."

"Could we take him out a little, on birds?"

I figured. It wasn't hardly hunting season, and anyway I could pretty well put the dog down where there weren't any birds to get into trouble with. It seemed safe enough.

"All right," I said.

The day was clear and cool for August, with the kind

of coolness that comes behind rains. The back roads were muddy, and I enjoyed riding in Jonathan's big car. We didn't have to go far. There was a long stretch of prairie, bright with goldenrod and asters and red sumac around the edges. The road was high enough so that we could see the cover all the way to the line of trees at the river; it was very pretty, but it wasn't quail country.

Psalmsinger was sitting in the back seat, pleased at being with Jonathan. We climbed out of the car and the dog danced around excitedly, the way the trial dogs do when they can hardly wait to run. And then I cast him off. He went down the embankment and out in the field with the kind of burning acceleration you see in a falling star, moving in wide, sweeping curves. But those lazy-looking curves are deceptive; Psalmsinger was weaving a splendidly efficient net across forty acres at a time and dredging the air for as far as we could see.

We walked behind the dog, the grass slapping wet against us, and Jonathan still in his business suit and low shoes, the meadow larks aroused by the dog flying up indignantly around us. Jonathan took off his hat and mopped his head with his handkerchief and kept saying, "Wonderful, wonderful."

At the brush that marked the river, Psalmsinger finally made game, but it was sure not to be a quail. He held, very staunchly and handsomely, but it took a long time for us to come up to him, and when I kicked around in front of him there was nothing.

Jonathan suddenly looked depressed. "Unproductive," he said. "So that's what he does."

"So do they all sometimes," I said. I sent the dog on, waving just the way my old man did, and Psalmsinger moved on a few feet, then he figured out what had happened and went downwind along the river for a hundred yards and swung back toward us, and that time he fixed his quarry with one of those skidding head-on points. This time we moved a little faster and a pheasant cock came out, full of rage and spread tail feathers and vocal bitterness.

"Well," Jonathan said. "It isn't *that*."

He seemed brighter. We went on back toward the car, and Psalmsinger hunted a mile very nicely, but there were no more birds. Once there Jonathan leaned against a fender, trying to get the weed seeds out of his pants cuff. Presently he said, "Tell me, boy, is it the gun that bothers him?"

"He's a good dog," I said. "Do you have a gun?"

"I would know you were related to your father," he said, but he grinned a little anyway. "Yes, I have a gun."

"Then get it out and see for yourself," I said. There was a tin can beside the road, and I went over and picked it up while Jonathan got his new gun out of its case. Then I tossed the can into the air.

Jonathan raised the new gun and pulled the trigger. The dog didn't flinch. Neither did the can.

"I was watching the dog," Jonathan said.

"Sure," I said. "And watch him this time, too."

He must have been watching the dog very closely. The can was unscathed. Then I put the can on a rock thirty yards out in the field. "Muzzle blast doesn't even bother him on the low shots," I said bravely. So far as I knew, Psalmsinger had never been within a country mile of a low shot.

Jonathan tried it again.

"You sure got the can that time," I said, lying as politely as I could. The grass had bowed down ten yards farther on.

"And Psalmsinger didn't blink," Jonathan said proudly. The big white-and-lemon dog sat looking at him with the gentleness plain on his face.

On the way back to the old place, the dog sat in the front seat between Jonathan and me. He was pretty muddy, and he didn't smell so good either. Jonathan did not notice.

My old man was waiting for us at home. He knew what we'd been up to, and I don't guess he liked it much. But Jonathan was busy talking to him, and they went in the house. I sat on the steps and Psalmsinger came and sat in front of me, a big, lovely, white-and-lemon dog, who had a heart I could not understand, but I knew it was a big heart. And I knew Jonathan was a good man; he had a big heart too, even though he couldn't shoot for shucks. No, he couldn't, for a fact; my old man hadn't exaggerated that a bit. I looked at the dog who grieved to see things killed and suddenly I felt fine, and the dog wagged his tail at me. That was the first time, too. I went into the house.

Jonathan was still talking, and my old man looked sort of serious. "I don't know," he was saying. "It's the boy's dog. Ask him. And ask him how much."

"Well?" Jonathan looked at me with that smile a man gets when he is very close to something. "How much?"

I took a deep breath. I said, "How much does it cost to go to college?"

After Jonathan and Psalmsinger were gone, sitting together in the front seat of the big car, both about equally muddy and smelling about the same, too, my old man and I stood together looking beyond the lawn at the tall grass.

"Don't spend the money yet," my old man said.

That's all he's ever said about it. But next fall I start college, so I guess it'll be safe to spend it soon. Jonathan and Psalmsinger have been together five years, and they are very happy. They hunt all fall in the North, and all winter in the South, and they have a wonderful time.

After all this time, I guess that even if Jonathan *should* hit a bird or two in the course of a season's hunting, Psalmsinger would forgive him for it, and perhaps not even feel too bad about it. The last time they stopped to see us at the old place, I mentioned that to my old man. He thought about it awhile, and then he said, "You going to college next fall?"

"Yes, sir," I said.

"Well, I'll tell you something that may help along the way," my old man said. "And this is what I'll tell you— that every good dog understands that a man can make a mistake."

"That is a saying mostly about dogs," I said, grinning.

"The devil it is," my old man said.

THE
CLAWS
OF
THE
CAT
Stuart Cloete

■

"I am old enough," the boy said.

"He is old enough," his father said from the bed.

"He's only twelve," the woman said.

"And I'm not afraid," the boy said.

"That's it," his mother said, putting her hand on his shoulder. "It makes me afraid that you are afraid of nothing."

"It's his blood," his father said. "He has bold blood from both sides."

"*Ja*, Jan!" the woman said. "And look where our boldness has got us. Because of it you are crippled."

"I shall get well," the man said. "The doctor has promised it. Besides, how could I refuse to ride the horse? If there had been no rain he would not have slipped and fallen on me."

"I have Moskou!" the boy said, pointing to the big hound. A bastard, the Boers called him, half foxhound and half collie. "And I have the gun."

"He's young to leave alone on the farm," the woman said again.

She looked round the kitchen. She looked at the door of the great oven where she baked bread, where her mother had baked bread before her. At the wood-burning stove, at the clay floors so carefully smeared each day with cow dung from the bucket outside the door. She looked at the wall recess that held the crockery. This was reality to her. All that was real in the world. Her home, her husband, her son. She had been born here and had never slept away from the place, except when they went camping each year by the sea, till she was grown up.

And now she must leave all this and go with her husband to Cape Town, to the hospital. The doctor had said she must be there, just in case. Besides, she knew that Jan would not be happy if she was not near him. Like a big black-bearded baby was this bold husband of hers. "Kaapstad, Cape Town," she said to herself. "And in a motorcar." She had never been in a car. But it would get them there in a day, and it would take five with horses. Besides, the horses had never been in a town any more than she had. And though she could drive them in the open veldt and over the mountains, she would be as frightened as they in a great town.

A bed had been moved into the kitchen, because it was easier to take care of her husband there. A man put his head into the half door, and said, "It is here." That was the motorcar.

"I do not hear it," she said.

"It's a new one," he said. "It moves very quietly."

"You have the gun," the man said.

"*Ja*, Pa, I have the gun."

The man and the boy stared at the old Mauser hanging from a nail on the wall. The nail was as old as the house, hand forged.

"And the dog," the man said.

"*Ja*, and the dog."

"And your blood that knows no fear," the man said. "The blood of the Swarts and the de Wets. A good cross," he said. "*Ja*, a good mixture like Moskou."

Two men came in, followed by the doctor. He said, "We'll take you now, Jan, if you're ready."

"I'm ready," he said.

The two men picked Jan Swart up. He was a big man and they staggered under his weight. His wife followed them to the car, and the boy followed his mother.

The doctor propped the sick man up, wedging him in the corner of the back seat. "Get in, wife," he said.

Jappie pushed past her to kiss his father.

"Do not fear for me," his father said. "I cannot die. I

can only be killed. It is not reasonable to think that I shall be the first of my race to die in bed like a woman. Fear nothing," he said. "And do what your heart prompts you, for through it courses the wild blood of your people."

"I shall fear nothing," the boy said. He backed out of the car, and his mother held him to her.

"Be good," she said, "and take care of yourself." She got in beside his father and wiped her eyes on a blue cotton handkerchief.

The doctor took the wheel. The car started.

The boy shouted, "Good-by, *tot siens,* till I see you."

"*Tot siens,*" shouted his father.

The car got smaller. In a few minutes it had stopped being a real car and became a toy. Then it stopped being even a toy. It disappeared behind a shoulder of the hill and was gone.

Then Herman Smit, the bigger of the two men, said, "It's gone. If you have any trouble, Jappie, come over to us."

His brother said, "Yes, come. And one of us will ride over every now and again to see how you are doing."

"*Baie dankie,*" the boy said, "very thank you, but I shall be all right."

"*Ja,* you will be all right," Herman said, "but all the same we shall come, for we are neighbors. And now we must go. It's a long walk back." The brothers laughed, because a walk of six miles over the mountains was nothing to them.

"*Tot siens,* Jappie," they said.

"*Tot siens,*" the boy said, "and *baie dankie* again."

He watched them go up the face of the hill, the pink heath closing about their knees as they climbed. They, too, got smaller and smaller. He saw them reach the top of the hill, where the white limestone was bare from the last-year burn. They turned and waved to him. Then their legs disappeared, their bodies, their heads. For a moment Hendrik's hat was visible, then that, too, fell below the ridge.

Now he was really alone. Moskou pushed his head into his hand. He reached a little higher than his hand, because without bending, the boy could hold his collar.

Moskou was yellow all over, a pale golden chestnut, lemon, as it is called, with a thick smooth coat, and eyes like yellow, black-centered agates. The only other black things about him were his wet nose, and the short hard nails of his round, catlike feet. He stood twenty-seven inches at the shoulder and had the legs of a foxhound. They were strong and straight, set on at the corners of his body. He appeared to have no hocks or pasterns, and his body was deep and thick. Round his neck he had a ruffle of thicker hair from his collie mother, but for the rest of him he resembled a great golden foxhound. As a matter of fact, his grandfather had come to Africa from a famous English pack, so there was good blood in Moskou. The blood that had hunted the fox and the buck for centuries, and before that had hunted the wild boar, the wolf, and the bear, when such hounds had been called St. Huberts, and England was still a forest.

His dam, the collie, was guardian of sheep, swift and vigilant, the servant and companion of man. And Moskou combined the qualities of his parents—the great speed, weight, and nose of his sire and grandsire, and the wisdom and affectionate nature of his dam.

Moskou was in his prime, four years old. His tail was slightly feathered and fastened strongly onto his back. When he was hunting, it lashed back and forth like a golden plume. When he got a hot scent he gave tongue, first whimpering, and then as the scent grew hotter giving his deep, bell-like bay, which in still weather would carry a mile or more over the mountains.

It seemed as if he knew his responsibility. As if he knew they were alone on the farm, the sole protectors of the homestead and the stock, because he came closer to the boy, his great shoulders rubbing against Jappie's thigh.

Alone, the boy thought, as he stroked the dog's head and gently pulled his ears. He was not afraid, but he was uneasy. It was a new experience and a great responsibility. He had been alone with his mother before, once when his father had been gone a week seeking a lost heifer. But quite alone like this he had never been, and the silence of the hills and their mystery fell upon him, covering him like a cloak. A green-and-scarlet sugarbird flew into the pomegranate by the orchard gate. It was like a jewel, he thought, that shone and sparkled in the light. Then it, too, flew away and the world seemed quite empty.

He thought of his mother and tears came into his eyes. He thought of how she had married his father. She had told him the tale many times. Of how he had come courting her on the strong wild horses he was breaking, and how her heart had fluttered like a bird in her breast when she saw this great bearded man on a big wild horse. Breaking and training horses and oxen for draft and saddle was his business and his pleasure. He was also a kind of vet, attending animals when they were sick and curing many of them with simple country remedies. He had a great way with dumb things, and his wife often laughed about it, saying, "I was as tame as a cow with that man from the first."

People paid him for his work in cash and in kind, but

mostly in kind, so that he had effects of all sorts on his place. Crippled animals that had been given to him, broken plows and carts, poultry, and the like, that he doctored up or mended and sold. People said, "If you can do anything with that, you can have it." And he took it, the plow or the mare. And he mended them, or fattened them, or tamed them, and out of them made enough to buy himself food and clothing; and what was more important to him, he had the friendship of all, for they sent for him only when they needed help and were always glad to see him when he came.

At first, though his coming had made his mother's heart flutter, she had not wished to marry him because of his wildness and his lack of education. But when she had inherited the farm, and he had said, "My heart, let us go into the mountains together and farm the place," she had agreed. Because otherwise she would have had to sell it, and big as it was—it was eight thousand acres—it was worth little, being all mountain, bush, and forest. A place only half tamed. But as he said, it was not right to sell the home of one's ancestors, the house where one had been born, when there was a man like him ready to help her with it.

His argument and the beating of her heart, which was never stilled when he was near, had convinced her. And for thirteen years they had lived on Baviaansfontein, Baboon Spring, and he had tamed it a little, building dams, clearing bush, and plowing patches of arable land that they had discovered among the trees and rocks. Little lands like big handkerchiefs dropped into the mountains from the sky.

And now all this was in Jappie's hands—the stock, four horses, six cows, four calves, eight oxen, one mule, a flock of twenty almost pure merinos, and the poultry. This was all they owned in the world. It was their capital and income. It had been won hardly. Bred, worked for, suffered for, and was, if lost, irreplaceable. It took nine months to make a calf. It took three more years to turn it into a cow, or four into a marketable ox. A horse could be worked at two, but was not at its best until five. And sheep, if they bred more quickly, died more easily. So that the flock they were trying to breed grew up more slowly than they had hoped.

Now, till his parents came back, he was the master of all this. The master, but also the servant. For man is the slave of the land and the beasts that require tending upon it. All must be watered and fed, cows must be milked, eggs picked up, sheep herded into their kraals at night, fences kept in order, and the weeds in the lands kept in check, before becoming so strong that they over-whelmed it. All, now, looked to him. It seemed to him that even the wheat in the land below the house swung in the breeze toward him saying, "Keep the beasts from eating us up." And the chickens walking on the short grass near the house said, "Protect us at night from the wild prowling things." A cow lowed in a field and her calf answered. And it was he who must bring the cow's overflowing udder to the calf's hungry mouth.

His father had said he was old enough, and he was. But only just. His father had said he must not be afraid, and he was not afraid. Not much afraid. His father had said he could count on the bold blood that ran in his veins, and his father never lied. But his blood and his nerve were untested, like a young soldier going into bat-tle for the first time. What he feared was fear; what he was most afraid of, was being afraid.

His work he knew. All of it, feeding, milking, herding, weeding. There was no work he could not do, save the heaviest, and that was not because of lack of knowledge, but because of lack of strength. All of it he had done many times before, but never with no one to talk to about it. This was the first thing he noticed. When he found that the black hen, sitting in a barrel, had hatched ten chicks, and he had put her in the big barn and given her water and mealies and bread crumbs, there was no one to whom he could say, "The black hen has ten chicks, and I have put her in the barn and watered and fed them."

He told Moskou, and Moskou wagged his yellow tail, and smiled up at him with open jaws. And so the first day went by, with all the work well done, and after cooking his mealie porridge and making coffee he went to bed in his father's bed in the kitchen. The comfortable smell of the man still lingered in it, and he lay with the dog stretched out beside him, and the Mauser leaning against the wall in the corner, and matches and a homemade candle on a shelf behind his head.

The next day passed quickly. There was no time to think till evening when all the work was done, and then he was too tired. All he could do was go over the day's work in his mind. Yes, everything was done. The cows milked, the calves shut in their hock, the horses watered and fed, the chickens shut up, the sheep counted and safely kraaled. He had cut wood for the fire in the morning. He had drawn a bucket of water from the fountain, bailing it out with a dipper from the cleft in the rocks that was worn with the steps of his ancestors' comings and goings, and the scraping of their vessels, as they had for a hundred years bailed the sweet fresh water from the rocky pool, into the buckets they carried into the house. The little path was worn deep with footprints so that it was a green, sunken ribbon that led from the house, past the bananas, to the hillside.

"Everything is done," he said aloud, and Moskou wagged his tail so that it thumped on the dung-smeared floor. Jappie was proud of himself. He had accomplished the work of a man this day. I am, he thought, a boy no longer, since I can do a man's work. The responsibility which had weighted him down disappeared, canceled by his ability to meet the demands which had been put upon him. He dreamed, half awake and half asleep, of the time when the twenty sheep would number a hundred, five hundred. When the six cows would be a herd of fifty, when. . . . And then he slept, his arm thrown out and hanging beside his dog's head. The dog licked his hand and then curled up beside him on the floor.

The next day Herman Smit rode over to see if he was all right. "*Ja*," he said, "I am all right."

"That is good," Herman said.

The boy put the coffee on the fire, and when he had drunk, Herman mounted and rode away.

When he had gone, Jappie almost wished he hadn't come, because a loneliness he had not felt before now descended upon him. Five more days went by, days filled with the work of the farm, the ministering to the beasts and birds that depended upon him, and upon which his welfare and that of his parents depended.

Then Herman rode over again. He said, "I have had news from the *dorp*. A man passed, Piet Fourie, with a message from your pa."

"My pa?" Jappie said, his heart almost stopped as he spoke. "He is well?" he asked.

"*Ja*, he is well. It is all over. They cut something in him. He has it in a bottle and is bringing it to show you."

"When are they coming?" Jappie asked.

"That is the message," Herman said. "They will be here Tuesday, if God is willing and all goes well."

"I will pray that all goes well," Jappie said. "I have prayed it every night and morning since they went away, but now I will pray more strongly." In his heart he had prayed already: Dear God, let nothing happen. Let them come back, for this burden is too great for a small son like me.

For though he was bold enough and unafraid with one part of him, the other part cried for the presence of his mother in the kitchen and the sight of his tall father working on the lands. The world was empty without them. Without the clatter of his mother's pans and the sound of her singing as she worked, and the shouts of his father to the horses as he plowed. They were sounds that were a part of his life, as much a part as the cry of the plover in the moonlight, the bark of the baboons in the hills, and the clattering cry of a bush pheasant when it got up in front of him with whirring wings. The sounds of his parents at work were a part of what his ears were accustomed to hearing, and the sight of them about the house and in the lands and fields helped to fill his eyes, rounding off, as it were, the landscape, giving it cause and reason.

"Today is Saturday," Herman said.

"*Ja*," Jappie said.

"There is Sunday," Herman said, "and Monday, and then they will be here, if God is willing."

"*Ja*," Jappie said, "if God is willing." To himself he said, "The day after tomorrow, I will be able to say tomorrow."

"If there is more news, good or bad," Herman said, "I will bring it."

Then he mounted and rode away, leaving a space behind him. A space that was filled by the thought that the
day after tomorrow he could say, "Tomorrow."

Sunday passed, also a working day for a boy alone, for
the beasts must be tended. But he read from the Gospel
of St. John, which was where his father had left off. Each
Sunday he read a chapter aloud, reading the Bible
through from end to end. In that Bible were the names of
his forebears, the dates of their births, marriages, and
deaths. It belonged to his mother, and he saw her birthday. She was thirty-one, and then he began working out
the dates on the calendar that his father had been given
by the storekeeper. Tuesday was the twelfth of Septem-
ber. It was his mother's birthday. That was a good omen.

He wished he could bake her a cake or give her some
gift. He generally managed to buy something. His father
used to take him to the store, ten miles away, for the
purpose. But now there was nothing he could do. He
could not leave the farm to ride twenty miles. It would
take too long. And then the violets came to his mind.
Some were in bloom by the pomegranate trees. His
mother loved flowers, and if he picked them now they
would last.

He went out to get them and arranged them in a glass,
with a border of their own leaves. Their perfume filled
the room. He set them on the little table by his parents'
bed, and he closed the door to hold in the scent. Then he
went to skim the cream from the milk he had set in pans
in the dairy that morning, and from there to the stable
yards and kraals to shut up for the night. It was a still
evening. Very beautiful, and all was well. He watched
the last bees coming home to the box hives. How late
some of them worked. And tomorrow, he could say,
"Tomorrow."

He was up before dawn saying it, "Tomorrow, tomorrow." He said it to himself, and then he saw Herman coming on his black horse. News, he thought. "Good or bad," Herman had said.

And the news he brought was bad. His father was wonderfully well, but they were not coming until Thursday, not for three days. Well, three days would pass, as the others had, but it was a blow to him. His mother would not be home for her birthday and the violets would not last. Still, there had been plenty of buds, and on Wednesday he would pick more. The days went quickly enough, because there was so much work. And the few days that separated him from his parents would go quickly too.

"You are a good boy," Herman said. "Your father will be proud of you, for it is not every young son who could have done what you have done. And many would be afraid."

"I have Moskou and the gun," the boy said.

"Nevertheless," Herman said, "many would be afraid. Why," he said, "many men would fear to be alone in so wild a place."

"It's my *woon plek*, my living place," Jappie said. "I know no other place, and I am not lonely with the animals and birds about me."

And again Herman rode away, but this time he left no space behind him; Jappie was getting used to being left alone. As he watched him go he saw the sheep coming in, led by Wit Booi, the big white *kapater*, the gelded goat. He had a bell fastened to a strap around his neck, and each evening he got a handful of mealies, as a reward for leading the flock home. Behind him came the ram and, strung out behind them, the ewes and lambs. That night Moskou was uneasy. He barked once and growled.

Jappie got up and, taking the gun from its nail, went out with the dog. But they saw nothing. All was still.

In the morning, when he went to the sheep kraal, one ewe lay dead. There was no mark on her, no blood. Perhaps she had died of illness, a sickness, but when they had come in last night all had been well. They had moved quickly and their eyes had been bright.

While he wondered, Moskou began to whimper. He went to the dog, and there on the soft ground outside the kraal was a spoor. It was big and round, a cat spoor, but nearly three inches across. "*Rooikat*," he said—lynx—and then, calling the dog to him he went back into the kraal and, parting the heavy wool round the ewe's neck under the yellow yolk that waterproofed her white skin, he found two tooth marks.

He dragged the sheep to the back veranda and, fastening a strap about its hocks, hoisted it onto a beam and made the strap fast. Later he would skin it and the meat would be good. But now he must make a plan. He worked quickly, milking, watering, feeding, and turning out the stock.

Plan? Before God, there was only one plan. He must do as his pa would have done. He must kill the lynx, for it would be back. There had been a shower in the night. The scent would be good and the spoor easy to see. He went into the house for the gun.

The boy went back to the kraal, patted Moskou and pointed to the spoor, saying, "Now go and find him and we will kill him, before he kills more of our sheep."

The dog put his nose to the ground. His tail lashed furiously, and then he was off at a canter. He went up the mountain, giving tongue. Jappie ran behind him. The gun was heavy in his hand, and the bandolier bumped up and down against his hip. He could hear Moskou, the bell-like note of his cry coming from not more than a hundred yards ahead, and then he came up to him. The hound had checked. Marking the place where he had lost the scent on a rocky flat, Jappie cast round in a circle with the dog and picked it up again. This time it was hotter and the hound went faster. The note of his voice deepened to a bay.

He is near, Jappie thought, and ran hard. Then in some heavy milk bush he heard Moskou barking loudly. He's treed him, he thought. Then came savage yelps and deep bays, as the lynx broke cover with the dog close behind him.

Jappie thought, He's seen me and he knows I can shoot him down from a tree. With the dog alone he would have stayed up there. The lynx ran up a steep cliff and turned into a small cave in the limestone. Now we've got him, Jappie thought, because Moskou was barking at the entrance and looking back at him as he climbed.

The cave gave onto a ledge, and as he reached it he saw the lynx crouched on the floor, glaring at him. Its great yellow eyes were narrowed slits, and its lips were drawn back over its bared fangs. Its red body was flat on the ground, its short tail raised. Its black tufted ears were laid back against its neck.

Jappie put up his gun and pulled the trigger. Nothing happened. He opened the bolt, reloaded, and fired again. This time the cartridge exploded, but as he shot the animal charged. The boy warded it off with the barrel, but the lynx bit him in the arm and scratched him from neck to belt with its sharp claws. He felt its breath on his face.

Dropping the rifle he gripped its throat, trying to keep it away from his face, and felt with his other hand for the knife in his belt.

As the lynx jumped at Jappie, Moskou had sprung at it, seizing it in the loin. The lynx turned away from the boy, as he stabbed it in the side, and swung back on the dog. As it turned, Jappie passed his hand over its back and drove the hunting knife in again behind its shoulder blade. Dropping him completely, the lynx fell on its back and, reaching upward, seized Moskou by the throat from below. The hound and the lynx became an indistinguishable blur of red fur and yellow skin. A spitting, snarling, growling, bloody mass.

Moskou shook himself free and stood over the lynx, his ruff covered with thick dark blood. With a savage roar he closed in again, his jaws on the lynx's throat. It was dead now, limp but twitching still. The hound stood over it for an instant, and then staggered and fell. Half skinned alive, the great muscles of his side exposed, one cheek torn out, he lay and, turning his golden eyes to Jappie, he died on top of the lynx. His eyes never closed, they simply lost expression, glazing slowly as death came to him.

Jappie sat down on the bloody floor of the cave. They had done it. The lynx was finished, but Moskou was dead, and without Moskou the lynx might have killed him. The dog had died so that he might live. He looked at his arm. It was badly torn and bleeding. He took off his shirt and cut it into strips with his knife and bandaged himself as well as he could. When he got home, he would put turpentine on it from the bottle on the shelf and cover it with cobwebs.

He was very cool now. He must fix up his wounds, and then fetch the dog and the lynx. He must come back with a horse. He went over the horses in his mind. There was only one, old Meisie, that was tame enough for the job. Horses did not like the smell of blood. He sat a little longer, and then took off his bandolier. It was badly scratched and had helped to save him. He laid it in a corner of the cave and stood the rifle beside it. His pa had said, "You have the dog and the gun and your blood." Now he had neither the dog nor the gun, but his blood had saved him, the fury of it that had boiled over when the lynx's fangs had broken the skin and muscles of his arm.

He went slowly home, his arm in a rough sling made from the rest of his shirt. At the house he took the brandy bottle from the cupboard and drank half a cup. He had never tasted brandy before, and it burned him, but made him feel better. Then he poured turpentine on his wounds. It bit him, stung like a hot iron. He walked up and down until the pain was less severe, and then, poking some cobwebs from the thatch, he covered the wound and bandaged his arm with the strips of old linen that his mother kept rolled and ready for accidents.

Now for Meisie. She was near the house and easy to catch. He bridled and saddled her. He got two *riems* from the wagon shed and led her up the mountain. Twice he had to rest. When he got near the cave, he tied the mare to a tree and dragged out the dead dog and the lynx. He succeeded in getting them onto a flat rock that was almost as high as the saddle. Then he took off his coat, covered the old mare's head with it, crossed the stirrup leathers, and hoisted the lynx from the rock onto the mare's back, tied it, passing the *riem* from its legs through the stirrup irons. Now for the dog.

As he tied Moskou beside the lynx he could hardly see for his tears. Then, taking his coat off the mare, he led her back. His mind was very clear. He knew what he must do. He knew he must do it quickly because as soon as he stopped he knew he could not go on. The cows. The cows must be allowed to run with their calves. He would not be able to milk. The horses could run. If the kraal was left open, Wit Booi would bring in the sheep. The poultry he would feed heavily, and then they must manage for themselves.

He offsaddled the mare, letting the saddle fall to the ground with its burden. Then he washed her back and flanks free of blood, because blood would cause her hair to come out. Then, running a *riem* through a pulley on one of the beams of the barn, he hoisted the dead body of the lynx and tied the end of the *riem*. It could hang there, beside the sheep it had killed, till tomorrow when his father came.

The grave for Moskou was another matter. It was hard to dig with one hand. He drove in the spade, pressed it home with his foot, and then scooped out the earth, levering the spade shaft against his knee. It was not a proper grave. It was more of a scraping in the black ground that ended, when he had dragged Moskou into it, as a mound beside the violet bed. That had been the only place to bury him. That he had been certain of since the beginning. There he would be remembered and safe.

With the grave finished, and the dog covered under a soft blanket of rich brown earth, Jappie dropped the spade and went into the house. He did not undress. He took off his shoes and fell on his father's bed. His father would be back tomorrow. Until tomorrow everything must take care of itself. He had done what he could and could do no more.

Not even with his blood could he do more. For a while he tossed about. Then he slept. Then he dreamed of his fight again, saw the green blazing eyes so near his own. Once more he saw the bared fangs, the white cheeks, the black whiskers, the tufted ears laid back, heard the snarls, and flung himself about in the frenzy of battle. Then he slept again.

His father looked about the room. The boy had not heard them come. "Where's Moskou?" he said.

His father looked pale and much thinner, Jappie thought.

His mother said, "What happened, Jappie?"

"Nothing," he said. "The *rooikat* scratched me."

"Lynx?" his father said.

"*Ja*," the boy said. "The lynx. We killed it. All is well but one sheep. He killed the sheep, Pa."

"And Moskou?" his father said again.

"Moskou is dead," he said. "I buried him. *Ja*," he said, "I buried him by the violets under the mulberry tree."

"A brave dog," his father said. "*Ja*, a brave dog."

"A brave boy," his mother said, stroking Jappie's forehead.

"*Ja*, he is brave," his father said, "but what else could he be with his blood?" Then he said, "How did you kill him, Jappie?"

"With my knife," Jappie said.

"But the gun? Surely you took the gun."

"I took the gun. But the shells are old, Pa. It misfired, and he charged. Moskou took him from behind, but he turned on him . . . and then I drove home the knife."

"I should not have left him," his mother said.

"He was big enough," his father said. "To kill a lynx with a dog and a knife is big enough."

"Moskou is dead," the boy said again, and turned his face to the wall.

"*Groot genoeg*," his father said. "Big enough."

THE
WOLF
OF
THUNDER
MOUNTAIN

Dion Henderson

■■■

All the way to the station my mother kept giving me the same instructions she'd been giving me for a week, because that was the first time I was allowed to take the train up north by myself to see Grandpa. Finally I reminded her how old I was, and then she said a funny thing. Growing up or growing old, my mother said, it doesn't make much difference how many birthdays you have. And all the way up north on the train I tried to figure out whether she was talking about me, or maybe Grandpa. The way things turned out, maybe she was talking about both of us.

At the Settlement, the train stopped just long enough to let me off and the conductor helped me with the duffel bag. It was so heavy I could hardly lift it, what with all the spare shirts and underwear and stuff my mother put in it. Then I looked around for Grandpa, but he wasn't there yet. It wasn't hard to tell. Grandpa was about nine feet tall and had eyes the same color as the barrel on the carbine, and one Saturday night he broke the big window in the saloon just by standing in the middle of the street and hollering at it.

The lumberjacks sitting on the bench in front of the general store watched me wrestle with that duffel bag and winked at each other, and when I got close one of them said did I figure I could stay overnight without any more gear than that. Now that was a pretty plain affront to my dignity, so I put the duffel bag down and said politely that I figured I had enough gear to spend a year on Thunder Mountain if I had to. "Thunder Mountain," one of the other ones said. He was kind of polite, too, all of a sudden. He said, "You the boy that goes up there to see the wolf?"

Well, I figured that was stretching it a little. Whenever I thought about that, the hairs stood up on the back of my neck and my hands got cold, but I couldn't let the lumberjack know that. So I worked up enough spit to spit on the board sidewalk that was all marked up by their boot corks and said, "That's the boy I am, all right."

They looked at each other as though maybe they felt something like I did, and maybe they did, at that, but it was for a different reason. Later on it turned out we meant different things when we talked about the wolf of Thunder Mountain. I meant the old gray wolf who got the moonlight in his eyes, and the people in the Settlement meant Grandpa.

But just then there was a commotion up at the end of the street, and the people on the sidewalk started to go indoors. One minute the kids and the farmers and the Indians and the tractor men and the lumberjacks were walking along the street, and the next minute the street was empty, and then I heard Grandpa. He was singing a Chippewa war song. My mother said his singing in Chippewa would raise the hackles on a cast-iron bear, but I kind of liked it even when I didn't know why.

Pretty quick he came in sight, driving the red horse on the dog cart. He never bothered with a car, because the first thing you had to cross on the way up the mountain was the Little Warrior, and he said he'd stick with the red horses until he found a car that could swim.

Right in front of me he stopped and looked at me and finished the last couple whoops of the song. Then he reached down smiling and picked up me and the duffel bag together and put us on the seat.

I said, "I'm glad to see you aren't real puny yet."

"How's that?" Grandpa said, and the new window in the saloon quivered a little.

"On account of what my mother said. My mother said you ought to come back down to the city with me this fall, because you're getting too old and puny to stay on the mountain all winter."

"Might have known it," Grandpa said. "Your mother's been saying that for thirty years." He smiled at me. "Tell her I said so. Tell her forty years, that'll fix her."

"My mother's only thirty-three years old last May."

"I know it," Grandpa said, smiling.

"Well," I said, "how's the wolf?"

"He's like me, boy. Gets older and maybe even a mite smarter, but no punier."

"Has he got a family this year?"

"No," Grandpa said, a little sadly. "Not anymore."

"Did you catch them?"

"I didn't fix to catch them, boy. But wolves are something like people. You fix to catch the smartest one of all, you have to catch all the young ones and the foolish ones and the ignorant ones first. That's what it is."

"Yes, sir," I said.

All of a sudden it seemed kind of cold. I guess I lived in the city too much, where people like my mother made a big fuss over a nosebleed. I knew that in the world, the real world, some things had to die so that others could live, but when I got right up against it, the day turned cold.

"Did you catch the puppies too?"

"No," Grandpa was a little short with me. He sounded disappointed that I'd asked. "I ain't caught a pup since that first one, and that was an accident. I caught the she-wolf before there were any pups."

"I suppose you had to."

"Yes," Grandpa said. "I had to. He brought her down off the reservation with him last year, and he showed me to her. Got so I knew they were following me and watching me, and the old wolf was saying to his mate,

See the way he does and learn all about him. Got so any time I circled on my own trail in soft going I'd find their tracks over the marks of my boots in the mud, the big one with the two toes missing, and the smaller one of the she-wolf."

"So you had to catch her, all right."

"Yes." Grandpa felt better because I understood. "The old wolf knew it and I knew it. I guess he knew how it would come out, too, but he kept hoping."

"Does he know you're going to catch him, too?"

"I couldn't rightly say," Grandpa said. "I reckon he figures there's some question about that."

"But you will."

"Yes," Grandpa said. "I got to."

While we were talking, the red horse was picking his way up the logging road that led through the Norway pine and spruce plantations, trees growing the way corn grows on farms. Pretty nearly forest size, they were, too. The cutters were taking a crop out of them every year, first the Christmas trees, then the pulpwood cutting that kept the plantations thinned out enough so the trees that were left could grow to timber. In my mother's time, these hills had been cut clean by the pirate loggers, left bare so you'd have thought nothing would ever grow there again. But times change. The trees came again in my time, more trees than there were before. Except on Thunder Mountain. Grandpa still had some of the old pines, the white pines that went up a hundred feet before they had a branch, as big across the stump as a house. We came to the stream, the Little Warrior, and there were some white stakes there where the logging road stopped.

"They wanted to build a road," Grandpa said, snorting. "I got a few pines up there, climax trees dying on the stump, and I calculated to move them down to the mill. But they wanted to build a road up Thunder Mountain to do it."

He meant the forestry people from the Settlement.

"What'd you tell them?"

Grandpa looked over at me and the dark blue eyes twinkled and he smiled.

"I told 'em quite a lot, far as words went. What it amounted to was that if any of them needed any toothpicks, they could come up and whittle them, one at a time."

Now we were across the stream, and the red horse was working hard, up the trail on Thunder Mountain. The white pines made a roof over us, a mile high it seemed like, and it was dark and cool down on the trail like you were in a cave or a church.

Grandpa said, "You can't change a place like this a little bit. Either you don't change it at all, or you change it altogether."

"Maybe," I said, "maybe they'll build the road while you're down in the city spending the winter."

"That'll be the day," Grandpa said. "When I go down to the city to spend the winter, they're welcome to build the road."

It appeared I said the wrong thing again. So I asked him to tell me about how he and the wolf first met, and how their war started. Grandpa said, pshaw, he reckoned I knew the story as well as he did, but I said, no, I'd forgotten some of it, and he said, pshaw, it wasn't much of a story, but I said, please, so he did.

Of course, that was five or six years ago, when it started, and the old wolf was a young wolf then, just another wolf. That was the spring there was no snow in the North country and the deer ranged widely from the yards where ordinarily they gathered in a herd so they could starve to death together after the cedars were browsed up beyond reach, and the wolf came down off the reservation early, following the deer. And although Grandpa didn't trap much anymore, even in those days, he saw the wolf's sign beside the body of a fawn deer and put out a trap, just to keep in practice, because in the days when he trapped seriously, he was the kind of trapper that some violin players are musicians. And the next day when he came back to the place where the trap was, he saw the wolf sitting there quietly, and it seemed to be the way those things always are. Wolves, the great wolves, those of the old forest in the North country, are very intelligent and it happens frequently that when a wolf like that is caught in a trap and he knows he is caught and determines that he can't escape, he won't struggle in a futile panic. Instead, he will sit quietly full of hate and wait to see the man who has brought him to the end of his splendid journey, and to hate the man fiercely but quietly until the very moment of death. Grandpa said he understood this very well, even though I didn't and if I was lucky I never would, but that he himself felt about the same way as the wolf did. The wolf, he said, looked at him unrelentingly while he prepared his revolver, a very handsome young dog wolf all metallic gray except for the black mask on his muzzle and the white-tipped ruff just behind his jaws. Then with the gun ready, Grandpa looked at the wolf for the first time personally, as an individual, and the wolf looked back at him fiercely.

But suddenly, as though quite satisfied that he would remember what he wanted to remember, the wolf came smoothly to his feet and with the magical wolf grace bounded beautifully and rapidly into nowhere—a bound one way, one another, and he was gone. He wasn't caught in the trap after all. But he had been, Grandpa said. The wolf had stepped in the trap and two toes of his forefoot still were there between the steel jaws. They were big toes, with strong curving black nails that showed the wolf was very strong and very smart and did not have to work hard to eat during an open winter when a common wolf might have worn his nails down to the toe in order to eat at all. Grandpa said he knew it would be different, trapping this wolf, because the wolf was different. The wolf had waited at the trap for him, to see the man who had trapped him so that he could recognize him again. And that was fair enough, Grandpa said, because the footprint with the toes missing let him recognize the wolf.

But they did not meet again, face to face, for a long time, although they came close. Grandpa watched the sign, and the cattle paths where the milk stock from the stump farms down the valley ranged, and the crossing places, and the wolf came back in twenty days. That was important information to him. The great wolves take command of space as large as they need to support their hunting, and they hunt it in a big circle so that they never deplete the game at any one place beyond the game's power to recover. And although Grandpa put out traps twice more that summer, he did not see the wolf again.

In the spring, though, the wolf brought a bride down from the reservation while there still was snow, and on the cold nights of late spring when a crust froze on the snow and gave the wolves good hunting while the deer broke through and wallowed helplessly, Grandpa would lie in his cabin and hear the signal yelps of the two wolves hunting. He did not worry about the deer, he said. There would always be deer. You could raise deer in a dog yard, if you had to. But in all the world there was room for only a few wolves.

Maybe he would not have trapped anymore for this wolf if it had not been for the people of the Settlement. Grandpa watched the moon and counted days and knew the weeks when the she-wolf would not run so fast, and the weeks she would not run at all, and the weeks when the pups would first be out. Not long after that, he said, the people from the Settlement came to see him. They stood a quarter mile down the trail and hollered and waited so that he would not shoot them or maybe scare them to death. There was a terrible situation, they said. A wolf pack had descended on the community. One wolf, Grandpa told them, and his mate and four pups. Well, the people from the Settlement said uncomfortably, anyway we have caught most of them. Yes, Grandpa said, you have caught three of the pups. Well all right, the people of the Settlement said. Will you catch the old ones?

That made it a matter of principle, Grandpa said. Once when there was a bear—no outstanding bear, in fact kind of a loutish bear by the best standards—they came and asked Grandpa, can you catch the bear? And Grandpa sat on his cabin steps smoking his pipe until the bear killed the only purebred Holstein bull in the county and they learned their manners. But now they were polite, and he put out his traps for the wolves. The pup was caught accidentally in a weasel set and drowned, and Grandpa felt so bad about that, that he stopped trapping for that year. The next year he caught the she-wolf before she had pups, but he did not meet the old wolf face to face again until the night I remembered.

Grandpa did not have to tell me about that again.

Maybe I was pretty young then, just a little boy you might say, but I remembered all right. I was in my bunk in the cabin, too excited to sleep, I guess, just from being there. The fire was almost out in the fireplace, but still I could see the furs on the couch, the silver foxes, and the big bearskin in front of the fire, and the moose antlers that held the rifles, and the color of the Bay blankets hanging on the wall, white with the candy stripes. I don't know, maybe I was asleep. But suddenly I was not asleep anymore. I was wide awake, straining my ears to hear something, and there was nothing. That was the trouble, there was no sound at all. There was silence all around, all the sounds of night in the forest around the cabin were silenced and somehow I felt cold.

I got out of my bunk and went to the door of the cabin and outside it was freezing still, no sound and the moon blazing down on the yard and the clearing as bright as day, but cold and still. I guess I didn't know enough to be frightened. But I went out on the porch and put my bare feet against fur, and when I bent over to look I saw it was Grandpa's cat. Dead. I looked around the clearing, and there at the edge the heifer was lying beside her block of salt and I walked over there, not feeling the wet grass cold on my feet anymore, and the heifer was dead, too. And in their yard, the geese too, the great Canadas that told about the coming of spring and fall, dead, dead, dead. I turned, suddenly frightened then, more frightened than I'd ever been, to run back to the cabin, but out of nowhere the wolf was there, in the yard, full in the moon, sitting between me and the cabin. I stood still and the moonlight was like ice running over me, and the wolf sat there and the moon was in his eyes.

I don't know what would have happened then, maybe I would have been like the cat and the geese and the heifer because by the wolf's reckoning I belonged to Grandpa too. But it did not come to that, because suddenly my grandfather spoke from the cabin, he spoke something to the wolf in his great voice, and the wolf, twice the size of a shepherd dog, turned smoothly and swiftly like water flowing to look at him, but in the same movement bounded toward the shadow. Then the carbine crashed from the porch, the splendid orange flower of fire so bright in the cold moonlight, and crashed again and the wolf fell heavily just at the edge of the shadows, and Grandpa came off the porch running. I tell you he was nine feet tall in the moonlight, running toward the shadows too, but the wolf was gone. Grandpa stood there with his rifle, and from the trees beyond the clearing the wolf talked back to him, the coughing, wailing lament that will raise the hair on people who don't even know what it is, not happy or sad or anything, but just the sound of death.

Grandpa said, I touched him that time, boy. And hearing his voice talking casually that way broke the spell and I began to cry, and Grandpa took me back in to bed and that's all there was to it, but I remembered that night without any trouble.

Now, riding up into the clearing behind the red horse, I recalled how frightened I had been and felt that I must be very strong and brave to make up for it.

Grandpa went and sat on the porch, and I unhitched the red horse and put him in the barn and rubbed him down. Then I said, "How about a trout for supper?"

"That's fine," Grandpa said.

"You want to catch him?"

"I believe I'll let you do it," Grandpa said.

The cabin was built of the white-pine logs, built into

the shoulder of the mountain as though it grew there, and the lancewood rod was where it always was. I found an early cricket in the woodbox by the hearth and went down to the pool where the Little Warrior came down the mountain behind the clearing. It was late afternoon, and cool. I put the cricket on the hook and tied a little stick on the line a foot above it, then let them into the pool gently without getting close to it myself. The current caught the stick and carried it down the pool, and I let out the line until the stick was through the little rapids, and then where the stream swung around past the roots of an old tree I twitched the line a little, and the stick came loose and the cricket sank in the clear, cold water.

And suddenly the rod bent and the line hummed, and I had a trout hooked. It took quite a while to land him, because I had to be careful of the old rod and the trees hanging over the stream, and then the rocks and the roots that the trout tried to get behind, but presently he was very tired and I led him to the edge of the pool where I could get him started fast enough to pull him up on the beach.

When I went back up to the cabin, Grandpa still was sitting on the porch. He looked kind of tired, but he admired the trout and said he believed he'd let me fix supper, too. So I cleaned the trout, getting the gills out neatly the way he'd showed me, and afterward I rolled it in cornmeal and fried it in bacon grease. I fixed some beans in the skillet, taking the bacon strips from the fish and putting them across the beans. I even ground some coffee in the old grinder on the cupboard and made coffee. My mother would have had a fit to see the way I fixed supper, but Grandpa said it was fine, and it tasted fine. For dessert I opened a can of peaches and we ate them out of the cups, then poured the coffee in with the syrup. After the first cup, we used honey for sweetening.

Right after we ate, Grandpa said he believed he'd go to bed, if I could clean things up.

"That'll be fine," I said. "I believe I'll sit up awhile, since all this here coffee'll probably keep me awake."

The red horse had to be fed and turned out, but there weren't any more chores outside. Grandpa never bothered to get another cat, or tame any geese, after the time the wolf was there.

When I was through, I built up the fire and sat down on the bearskin and looked around at the things in the cabin, the things I remembered like the antlers of the buck deer locked in combat the way they died and the Siamese fawns and the white robin Grandpa had mounted, and I drank three or four cups of coffee and I figured I'd stay awake for a week.

Next thing I knew it was morning and the fire was out. Grandpa was still sleeping. That was kind of funny. When I stopped to think, I didn't remember ever seeing Grandpa asleep before. But by the time I had the fire built up and breakfast ready, he was sitting on the edge of the bunk. He still looked tired.

"Reckon I won't eat any breakfast just now," he said. Then he looked at me, and I must have had some sort of expression on my face, because he said hastily, "Well, maybe just a mite. Always was partial to trout for breakfast."

But he didn't eat much, and when I finished he looked at me with those gun-barrel-colored eyes, and said, "I believe you'll have to go out and look at a couple of traps this morning."

"Yes, sir," I said. "Where are they?"

"Well, I'll draw you a kind of map," Grandpa said. "There are only two, over by the crossing place on the north fork of the Little Warrior."

"Wolf traps?" I asked eagerly.

"Yes. Wolf traps." Grandpa smiled at me. "I calculate the old wolf was going to cross that way last night, crossing by the place where the burned log lies partly in the stream. I calculate he passed there last night, and he won't cross there again for a year."

"He won't?"

"No," Grandpa said. "I understand him. To understand a wolf, you need only to think like a wolf. And me"— Grandpa smiled at me—"I have had more experience than the wolf has. That is my advantage."

"All right," I said. "If you will draw me the map."

"Be careful," Grandpa said. "You haven't had hardly any experience thinking like a wolf at all. One trap is in the trail, and you may find a hare in it. No wolf, even a young and foolish one. But there is another set, above the first, where a wolf might go in order to inspect the trap in the trail. You must be careful not to step in that one yourself."

"Yes, sir," I said. "I'll bring them back."

"No," Grandpa said. "Spring them and leave them."

That was when I realized that Grandpa was sick. "Leave them?"

"Yes," Grandpa said. "If I have not caught him now, I will not try again. The wolf and I are both growing old. And maybe"—he smiled at me—"maybe as your mother says, puny."

I said, "Before I go to the traps, I could ride up to the reservation and find Doc Champion."

"First the traps," Grandpa said. "First the traps, later something else."

He was very firm. I took the map and saddled the red horse, then came back into the house for the carbine. Grandpa was lying down again. I paused, worried, and he did not open his eyes, but he said, "First the traps."

So I went to the traps. Partly I could ride, then the trees closed in and I walked for a while, leading the horse. It was a good thing I was leading the horse when we got close to the traps, because suddenly he snorted and reared and almost pulled the reins out of my hand. I pulled, but the red horse stood trembling and snorting, so I tied him to a tree and went on to the crossing place.

And there was the wolf, waiting, the old gray wolf with the black mask and the white streak across the top of his head that must have been from Grandpa's bullet. He looked at me the same way he had looked that night when the moon was in his eyes; but he looked surprised to see me. His foreleg was caught deeply in the trap; there was no use struggling and he hadn't struggled. He had been lying down in the grass waiting, and the grass was bent down there, but there were no signs of useless struggling. I looked at the wolf and my hands were sweating so I almost dropped the carbine, and when I brought it up I could not hold the barrel steady until I braced it against a tree. The old wolf sat there with his leg in the trap, looking at me with that strange expression, surprised at seeing me instead of someone else. He did not believe it when I brought the barrel steady on him, he did not believe any of it, not the trap nor the gun nor me nor the shot either. He did not believe any of it at all, and then he was dead.

I saw him lying there and smelled the powder smoke, and I did not believe it either. I went over and touched him with my foot and turned his head, and then I saw his eyes and I believed it. The eyes did not hate anything anymore.

Afterward I went back for the red horse, but he did not want to come very close. I took the rope from the saddle and tied it to the wolf and tied the other end to the saddle. I could not get the red horse any closer than that to the wolf, even if the wolf was dead. The red horse did not believe it either. That was how we got back to the cabin.

Grandpa still was lying down on his bunk. Without opening his eyes, he said, "Was there a rabbit in the lower set?"

"Yes," I said. "And the wolf was in the other."

"Yes," Grandpa said. "To be sure."

"Really," I said. "The wolf."

"A wolf," Grandpa said, opening his eyes that were the color of the carbine barrel. "Some wolf."

"No," I said. "The old wolf. With the two toes missing and the bullet mark on his head."

Grandpa smiled at me. "You have run too hard beneath the spring sun. You are not used to running uphill."

"The old wolf," I said passionately. "He was in the trap."

"No," Grandpa said. He sat up suddenly on his bunk. "No. Not after all this time."

"Yes," I said. "It was just the way you said. He was caught in the trap when he went to look at the place where you put the other trap."

"All right," Grandpa said, looking hard at me. "Now I believe you. Where is he now?"

"He's out in the yard. I had to drag him behind the red horse. I thought you would want to see him."

"Drag him," Grandpa said, the beginning of a strange expression on his face. "He is not dead?"

"He is dead all right," I said. "He did not believe and the horse did not believe it and you do not believe it, but he is dead all right."

"No," Grandpa said. "He can't be dead."

The expression was getting clear on his face now.

"He is dead as anything. If you will come outside you can see him."

"No," Grandpa said.

I started to say something, then I saw quite suddenly the expression on Grandpa's face. He was not looking at me now. He was looking beyond me, out through the door, out over the dropping lines of the ridges leading away from the mountain, just showing the blue haze of new candles on the pines. Above the mountain there was a thin clean marking of geese against the sky, and the sound of their calling, so faint you did not know whether you heard it or remembered it from another time.

"I'm sorry," I said to my grandfather, without knowing why. "Did I do something wrong?"

"No," Grandpa said. "No."

"Should I have let him go?"

"No," Grandpa said.

"Maybe I could have let him go."

Grandpa said, "He did not ask you to." It was a kind of a question.

"No," I said. "He looked at me with his teeth showing, he looked surprised."

"Yes," Grandpa said. "All right. He was old then, but not too old."

I didn't understand him.

"You must not worry," Grandpa said. "It will be a long while before you need to worry. But neither a man nor a wolf should get too old."

"I didn't mean to do wrong."

"You did very well," Grandpa said. "You mustn't worry. But perhaps you will bury him now."

"All right," I said. "But shouldn't I go for Doc first?"

"No," Grandpa said. "Maybe after you bury the wolf, you will hitch up the red horse, and we will go down to the Settlement."

"Do you think that would be best?"

"I believe it would," Grandpa said. "I believe maybe your mother knows best."

"You mean about how you're getting—" I couldn't say it.

"Maybe she does," Grandpa said. "Maybe I ought to go back to the city with you, after all."

For a little while I didn't say anything. Then I said, "She didn't really think you'd come. She didn't think you'd leave the mountain."

Grandpa lay back on the bunk. He was smiling. "Things change, boy."

He looked at the ceiling, still smiling. "You come back here, boy, when you're grown up. There'll be a road. And the pine'll be gone. And you know what?"

I didn't say anything.

Grandpa said, "There won't hardly be a mountain anymore."

He lay there and I went out and buried the wolf and hitched up the red horse. Afterward I went back and helped Grandpa out of the cabin and into the dogcart. He wasn't really nine feet tall. All the way to the Settlement I kept one arm around him and did my best not to cry.

OLD
JASPER
AND
THE
FOX
TELLER

Paul Annixter

■

■ ■ ■

One spring morning Jasper, the wily red fox of the Santee River country, lay in the couchlike crotch of a fallen sweet-gum tree. His sharp chin rested on his paws, his eyes were closed, and he looked like a reddish burr caught in the arching limb. He was asleep there in the fine spring sunlight, but the breeze that drew up from the river woods stroked his nose, and that nose, second to none in all the wild, was as keenly at work as when its owner cruised the woods. Likewise the cocked and pointed ears.

It was just the right weather for an old dog fox to cover ten or twelve miles of rock and scrub and alder vale for a spring checkup, and such a foray Jasper meant to take when he had made up for the swift-moving night of raiding just passed. The spirit of romance was keen in his blood these days, and somewhere out there among the pine-clad hills an unknown mate awaited him.

All winter he had made his trails alone and snarled at the approach of any of his clan. But with the first scent of new green and fresh mold riding the March breezes, old habits were forgotten, and trails and runways were a-patter with many feet scurrying on the errands of spring.

For three years Jasper had denned in a sumptuous stronghold of several corridors, dug deep into a hill by more than a century of fox generations. Here he might have slept in utter safety, but he eschewed the aches of den damp with encroaching years and craved the sun.

He was a splendid specimen of his kind with a rich ruddy pelt that made golden streaks across the hills as he pursued his prey. His dainty feet and legs were black, his brush was a magnificent vanity that swept the ground, he had remarkable speed and eyes that fairly snapped with intelligence. He was the wiliest fox the Santee River country had ever known, and men had honored him with a name. He was known at least by word of mouth to every hunter in four river counties. Time and again men had matched their wits against him and lost. The cunning pointed mask of Jasper when he turned in his tracks, continued to grin back at the best trailing dogs the hunters could gather, but never from wall of hunter's living room.

Jasper loved to tease the mongrel packs of the hillmen. In his patrician heart dwelt a profound contempt for all of them, an abiding confidence in his own superior wit, his knowledge of the dim and difficult ways they could not follow. It had become but a pleasant recreation for him to wind and thread his way around the mountainside until the ill-assorted packs of coon and bird dogs became separated, and then to watch from some promontory as the blundering brutes went plodding home at nightfall, tired, footsore, and sorry. His tricks were legion—a new one for each occasion. Times he would choose the steep flinty paths until the dogs would give up and turn back with cut feet. Again he would run a labyrinth of fallen trees in the swamp woods and watch from a hill to jeer fox talk at dogs and hunters as they emerged from the woods, mired to the hips.

It became rumored in time that Jasper could not be caught. He had played with packs so long he had become almost a legendary figure. But other foxes in the region had suffered under the continuous hunting. The foolish grays had all but been exterminated, and the reds were thinning fast. Jasper's mate had fallen to the hillmen, likewise his son, who, young and conceited, had tried to emulate his father's example and devil the dogs at close range. Without Jasper's leathery lungs and seasoned wile he had holed in the rocks and been done to death.

And then a new hound had come into the region, a true fox teller, slow, but a faultless tracker, owned by Whit Turner of Alderside, and Teller he was called. A crossbred coonhound, named for his specialty with foxes, he had been Jasper's special enemy for the past year and had come to constitute his particular and specific nemesis. An old hound, this Teller, his seamed and lop-eared face scarred by battles, his sprung joints and gnarled and broken nails testifying to the endless trails he had traveled. Slow he was compared to most dogs, his haw eyes red and none too sharp—all his other senses subordinated to his nose. But that nose was the coldest that had ever run the Santee trails and knew no other scent once it was laid to a certain track. The track might be a day old, but Teller would follow on relentlessly. He was the one dog in the region Jasper really feared.

Twice in the past six months he had run Jasper's trail, unraveling all twists and tricks for a younger, swifter pack. The last hunt had been but a week before. The hunters had left the swamp woods with another red fox, Jasper escaping by only a narrow margin. That run had been too close and too long for the old fox's liking. Life for him had taken on a serious note of late.

About midmorning Jasper ended his beauty sleep. His ears pricked straight up and his eyes opened, though he did not move otherwise. A faint long-drawn sound that started echoes along the hillside had come to him on the breeze, a wailing note at first, broken through by deep-toned bellows, booming and sinister. The trailing chorus of a dog pack. And somewhere behind the dogs were men.

Jasper sat up and waited the clearer story, waited for a voice he knew—the voice of Teller—and as he waited a flea bit him and he rubbed his ear like a cat with a front paw. He had been expecting another hunt; it was quite in order after his many chicken raids on the settlement farms. No proof yet that it was his trail they were on, however. Jasper was still quite unconcerned. His mouth was open, and he seemed to grin.

Nearer came the hound chorus. He could hear the high eager babble of the younger dogs. The sounds would burst out clear and sharp as the pack crossed the rim of a hill, then sink to a murmur as they dipped into some distant valley. A good mile away. Quite possibly it was he they sought. He was the fox that had shamed them the most. He was beginning to feel something wrong now, through his vague fox sense which men called instinct.

Sudden silence. They had lost the scent for the time being. The young and blustering mouths were stilled. Then one voice took up the cry, belling *Ooowah, Ooo-wah.* How Jasper instinctively hated the sound of it. Somehow it made the hair on his roach stand erect. Then the full cry of the pack again along the swamp trail. Anxiety was just beneath the cloak of his self-confidence now, yet no pack had ever filled his heart with actual fear.

He made off down the hill, a golden streak amid the brush. He was heading directly toward the oncoming hounds, looking sharply about for strategic aids as he went. Presently he dove into a faint cane-lined trail he knew. Soon he had maneuvered well behind the dogs, by a way that led through foot-deep water. This was only one of the many wiles he knew for confounding a pack, but at present there was no great need of exerting his wits.

Still smiling and lolling his tongue he sat listening to the hue and cry as the dogs churned about the bed he had left. Then a baying told they had picked up his fresh trail. The cries became an unearthly outburst of sound, but in less than half an hour he had them guessing again. The short frenzied yaps that meant fresh trail were silenced, and only a broken clamor rose now and again from the younger dogs, whose tongues were keyed to their emotions and lied more than half the time. Jasper knew them all, recognized them one after another—the two lumbering coonhounds, the locally bred foxhound, Luch; the Airedale, Toby. He paid no heed to these, he waited for the voice of Teller, now silent.

He heard it presently, deep bugle notes. No lie or indecision there. Time for a new trick. Up out of the swamp Jasper streaked, threading a laurel slashing toward dry stony ridges, which would not hold foot scent long. He swerved westward toward a meadow from which the strong odor of sheep came down the breeze. Old Jeff Keyser's flock, more than two hundred head, were stampeded from their browsing a few minutes later by a reddish form that leaped upon the stone wall at the pasture edge, ran it for fifty feet then sprang well out into their crowded midst. As the sheep rushed headlong across the pasture, the old fox ran nimbly in their midst, knowing that his own scent would be almost entirely obliterated by the pungent odor of the fold.

Then he made straight for Bee Rock, a promontory of rock five hundrd yards above, named for the many wild bees that nested in its crannies. Straight past the rock he ran for a hundred yards, returned in his own tracks to the base, sprang to a ledge of the rock. From there he took a long leap out and downward so that he cleared twenty feet or more before he landed in thick laurel. Then off along the hillside he streaked.

Such tricks would have baffled any ordinary pack, but

old Teller would work them out, he knew. However, there was time now to rest and figure. He headed for a distant earth he knew. He did not hurry and frequently sat down, red tongue dripping sweat, ears pricked for news. It would take time to untangle the snarls he had left, but somewhat later he looked down from a rocky cattle path and made out old Teller working the puzzle out in his own wonderful way, while the young dogs milled about, sterns a-quiver. Then the hounds' chorus swelled again.

Jasper did not know that the original pack had been strengthened by two new and experienced dogs; and that Whit Turner and four other hunters, all long-suffering poultrymen, were behind the pack, bent on reparation if the hunt took two days. But he did sense that he was in for a bitter duel that would take all his wile and strength to win.

The whole forest world was on edge by now. He passed Wizzle, the old possum of Wyble Woods, chattering dry, gnomelike curses as he swarmed up a tree, fully believing his last hour had come. Noon—and the pack was much closer. The two new dogs were a menacing addition. Dogs from all the surrounding country were coming in now to join the chase. Jasper was a bit worried. Unknown to him a younger fox, a compatriot of his, less schooled and wary, had been holed and killed. The hunters were not interested in the young fox. He was not the infamous Jasper and meant little one way or another.

In the early afternoon the old fox led the chase straight up the highest hill of the countryside, choosing the steepest, rockiest gullies to the crest. Those old dogs, he saw, could not be deceived for an instant, but this high country would be ideal for his next aim, which was to tear the heart out of the belling gang behind, lame them and cut their pads on flint and rubble. Once on the crest Jasper ran round and round the flat summit. Twice he leaped down the slope a ways, returning carefully in his own tracks. Then he lay resting as he watched the dogs laboring up the gulley below, fairly shaking the ground with their outcry. Thirteen of them now, and there like specks far down at the swamp's edge, the hunters moved.

He waited till the dogs had almost gained the summit, then dropped down another gully and heard them raging about the summit. Some of the younger dogs were fooled by the false trails he left and were away down the hill. Good! Perhaps he had outwitted them at last. But no. *Ooowah, Ooowah.* The long quavering wail of Teller drew them back. The pack answered, rounding back to his fresh trail again.

Uneasiness was growing in Jasper now. Formerly he could have secured rest or definitely baffled pursuit by crossing the trail of some other fox and leaving it to draw the dogs. But that time had passed with the coming of Teller. Midafternoon heat was telling on him after his long run. But he must go on.

Down into the river woods again, to lay a tangled trail among ponds and slimy mire. Then to an amphibious spot of down timber where sunlight never filtered and fat fungi grew in profusion among the rotting logs. Through the thick of these he ran raising a mist of dry impalpable dust. Long ago he had learned that the taint of the fungi overpowered the scent of any animal. Half a dozen foxes might have sat in that area and not been smelled.

Nearby was an ancient oak, long dead, hollow and half barkless. Along its trunk clear to the bare sapless branches the tough leathery fungi grew. Into an opening at the base of the trunk Jasper slipped with an air of familiarity, and a minute later he might have been seen peering from another shadowy opening near the top. Here even Teller's nose would be powerless. Only human ingenuity could discover him here.

He waited trembling, till the pack came stringing up, stopped and swarmed in a many-colored wheel, nose hubbed. The trail cry broke to a disrupted babble as the young dogs yelped their perplexity over the suddenly vanished scent. Back and forth they wove like wound-up toys not yet run down, coughing over dust of wood rot and puff ball.

Up above Jasper peered forth and grinned. And dust was his undoing, for one of the hunters, Lem Sproal, had just come up with the pack. Fifty yards away he stopped in his tracks with an ejaculation that will bear no recording. He had just seen the mask of the old fox protrude from the hole in the dead tree. Lem's rifle rose, and he almost forgot in that moment the time-honored law of the fox hunt, that only the dogs shall do the killing. Jasper saw the lifted gun. A golden streak shot out over the heads of the astonished dogs, a leap of fully twenty-five feet, and an instant later the woods had swallowed him.

With a roar the dogs were off again. With his prize strategy discovered, Jasper gave up all further effort at evasion. Every trick he had tried had been unraveled as if it did not exist; Fate seemed to have turned her face from him at last. Desperate now, he simply ran, though he was already far gone from the terrific pace he had set. He had strained himself to the utmost in executing his strategies while the pack had taken a normal pace.

From that time on Jasper labored on through a hell of a thousand years. All the rest of the long hot afternoon he ran in growing misery and actual fear. Sometimes he would follow a creek bed for a time or plunge through thickets of tangled briar which would lacerate the tender hide of the short-haired dogs. But a respite of a few minutes did not rest him now. He would stiffen in the muscles at the first bit of inaction. His body would flounder, leap, and roll without apparent reason as he started on again from the numbness creeping up his legs.

Down into the gloom of the swamp again, drawn by need of water, for his fine coat was plastered brown with sweat by now, his tongue lolled far out and slavered over his grinder teeth. Down through alder, cane and sedge, to pause belly down to lap and wallow in the muddy water.

He had never been in worse distress; his heated blood beat in a sickening pain against the base of his brain; his soaked brush drooped with the weight of mud clinging to its plume and grew heavier as he went. He thought of his home den amid high rocks, but gave up the idea of reaching it. If he did, the world would be howling about his walls in no time. There would be pick and shovel and smoke and hounds' paws to unearth him. The whole region was forbidden ground to him now, for he could not hope to weather such another ordeal as this. Teller and the pack were too trailwise to be beguiled again; they could not be deceived. If he escaped at all now, it must be to new territory.

Five o'clock found the hounds less than two hundred yards to the rear. Jasper, mired in a swampy pond, was so weak he could scarcely flounder out. Only by seizing a vine in his teeth did he manage to heave himself free, to find the dogs almost within sight. Too gone even to shake himself, the old fox stood still with lowered head and mouth opened in a grin of pain instead of craft, until the dogs actually saw him. It looked as if he were done and

would face them there, but the water had refreshed him
a bit. Away he streaked, and the tired hounds had a turn
in the mire.

The long dusk began and still that never-ceasing
bay behind. A fiend's cry for his life, now that he had
shown himself to them. Red mists swam before the old
fox's eyes. Times he would lapse into complete uncon-
sciousness while still struggling on. He could not hold
out much longer, and the dogs knew it. The hunters
themselves had come in close in the past hour, and now
and then Jasper heard a shout as one of them signaled to
another.

Startled birds voiced their protests as the old fox
floundered through the thickets. Down in the south, heat-
lightning flames flashed above a low bank of clouds.
There was a smell of rain in the air, but it would not
come for an hour or more. Too late to blot out Jasper's
trail. Too late to save him.

Down toward the river again. Jasper hadn't realized he
was so near the stream till now. Possibilities here if he
could increase his lead enough. Had he been fresh he
might have swam the stream, but the river was wide and
he was too far gone. Folly to think of that.

As he reached the bank a hunter emerged simulta-
neously from the woods and stood peering. Jasper
whisked to cover again, and the dusk saved him. One
more double and he was behind the blundering hunter.
Down to the water he slipped, and as he bent stiffly to
lap he fell forward into the stream from sheer exhaustion.
He paddled against its flow for a few moments, then gave
up and just drifted with the current. It bore him slowly
downstream, and he lapped as he floated. In his great
fatigue he gave himself over, decided to struggle no
more, just drift forever in the cool waters. The hounds

might tear and eat him if they would. Then the splashing and panting of thirteen heavy-breathing dogs only a few hundred feet upstream roused him, and fear returned, fresh will to live.

He sank until only the black tip of his nose protruded. He heard with exultance the retreating whimpers among the thickets and softly paddled on. The deepening dusk was with him. Then a shadow came running downstream and spoke of the scent of Jasper at the spot he had entered the water. Teller, the faultless! A baying from twelve splashing hounds gave answer. Upstream and downstream they swam while the old trailers counseled from the bank and the voice of a hunter spurred them on.

Until nearly midnight they continued to draw the woods in ever-widening circles, but never a further trace did they find. At last, when the late moon rose behind the swamp trees, the hunters grudgingly admitted defeat. The old fox had outsmarted them again, though no one could figure it out.

They did not know that Jasper had swum straight out into midstream, without thought or care of life, and that just before his strength gave out, the little river steamboat that plied past once each day had rounded a bend in the stream. As usual, the steamer had a freight barge in tow. As the boat chugged past within twenty feet of him the old fox with a final effort overtook the barge. An end of rope hung trailing in the water, and this he seized in his teeth and, unknown by any, was towed away down river.

For nearly an hour he rested thus while the steamer bore him on. Later, some six miles downstream, he struck out for land again, swimming strongly once more. He gained the shore and plunged into the fastness of another swamp, far from the range of his old enemies. Morning found him nursing his aching muscles in a new, warm den beneath the buttressed roots of a sycamore. In a day or so he would be himself again, but never again would he bedevil the poultry farmers round Wyble Woods.

THE
BLAZING
STAR

MacKinlay Kantor

■

■■■

This happened out in our country a long time ago. Maybe Judge Sheffield wasn't so old in those days, but they called him Old Judge Sheffield on account of the ponderous way he walked and the ministerial voice he had. But many people swore that Nathan Sheffield was a boy at heart. I guess a man wouldn't go hunting squirrels unless there was some boyishness in his nature, and that's what Judge Sheffield did on the day that he first saw the quilts and felt their beauty with his hands.

Up into the Glencoe neighborhood was where he traveled, a good ten miles northwest of Minnehaha, and considerable distance to drive behind a sedentary horse like Old Dick.

He tied Dick against a timber fence near the Chicken River. He took his rifle and walked amid the walnut trees. Thin and yellow the leaves shone against the autumn sky, and you could hear crows bickering all through the fragrant bottomland. There was a taste of frost in the air and the taste of red haws in Judge Sheffield's mouth. Now and then his nostrils sucked in the wild, cool, smoky smell of prairies that burned in the afternoon sunlight, north and west for a hundred miles.

This was Judge Sheffield's way of worshiping God, and he didn't really care whether he got a squirrel or not. He used to be quite a commanding figure in church, and he even taught the Junior Baraca class; but plenty of autumn mornings his soul was up and gone among the walnut trees.

Well, he had the pleasantest afternoon possible, but when he came whistling back through the first blue dusk, he was treated to a surprise. He had expected to find Old Dick tied and contented, and the buggy waiting. Neither the buggy nor Dick was to be seen.

Judge Sheffield pondered, and was annoyed, because

he had looked forward to an easy drive, and now it looked like a tramp of three hours. Buggy marks led across the colored, fallen leaves into the road. Old Dick had gone to his barn in Minnehaha, just as he always did if he were untied, for he was a kind of independent horse.

Just then, as the Judge always told it, he heard turkeys over across the river—not wild turkeys, but the barnyard kind. So there was a house not far away, and maybe he could get a bite to eat before he took out for home.

As he turned to walk toward the bridge, a big man came out of the woods and crawled between the fence rails. The face of the man was familiar to the Judge, not this particular face, but one like it. He could see it plainly, a big, vacant face, redder than the hillside oaks and a good deal more surly.

"Hello," said Judge Sheffield. "Did you happen to see a white horse hitched to a single buggy with the top down? He was tied up to the fence."

The young man was fleshy. He was about twenty-five. He stood and grinned down at Judge Sheffield, though the Judge was no little man. "Who had the top down, Mister? The buggy or the horse?"

The Judge shot fire out of his eyes. "Young man," he said, "you look like a Heffelman to me."

"That's right, Judge," the fellow said with a smirk. "I'm Anson Heffelman."

Judge Sheffield said gravely, "You know me then. Maybe you know my old horse Dick. I left him tied this afternoon, but he seems to have strayed away. I'm afraid that he's gone home without me."

"That's just too bad," said young Anse Heffelman, and he went away up the road, swinging the bucket he was carrying.

Well, the Judge looked after him and shook his head. He had a good notion who had untied Old Dick from the fence post, and it seemed a mean trick to play, especially if the prankster knew, as most of the county did know, that Dick would march for home the moment he was given a chance.

The Heffelmans were like that. The old man was coarse and mean; doubtless his offspring were meaner. Judge Sheffield kept walking. His feet resounded on the log bridge across the Chicken River.

There was a house beyond the stream. It wasn't much of a house; but blue smoke came from the chimney, and as the kitchen door swung open the red eye of a wood range beamed out. The Judge wiggled his nose and thought how steak and gravy might smell if they were preparing themselves upon that stove. He turned in at the gate, where a friendly shepherd dog rubbed against him. He hallooed, and Widow James came at his call.

She was a little woman, the widow. Sheffield didn't remember her, but later he recalled that a fellow named J. O. James had fallen through the ice up there on the Chicken River a couple of seasons before and got himself drowned. This was the widow he had left, and with her appeared two young sons.

The widow had started having sons pretty late in life, or else maybe she was worn down and aged by work and worry. She was short and round-shouldered, and her tanned face was a mass of lines. The same acts of God and fortune that put those lines in her face had thinned her hair and bleached it white. She had bright brown eyes that looked quizzically out from under wide, curving black brows. She wore a ragged coat, a man's coat, for she was busy with her poultry when Judge Sheffield came.

He made known his situation, and he didn't even have to hint about supper.

"Land alive!" she said. "I don't know whether we can set a very presentable table for you, Judge Sheffield, but we'd be tickled to death to try. It isn't every day you get to sit down with a distinguished judge."

The two young boys stood aloof and maybe a little frightened, but pleased withal.

"George and John, these are." She introduced them. "George is fifteen, and John's thirteen and a half. My eldest ain't home yet. He's off a-hunting, as usual, but he'll soon be with us. Jim-Jim, he is."

Judge Sheffield repeated "Jim-Jim," and wondered at the name.

"I guess it's on account of we're Welsh," said Mrs. James. "We called our eldest James, for his first name, and that's a fashion amongst Welsh people. My own grandfather's name was Lewis Lewis, but we've always just called our eldest Jim-Jim. Now you come in and sit yourself down."

Judge Sheffield wouldn't have anyone make company out of him if he didn't want to be made into company. Despite anything the widow might say, he chopped wood for her kitchen fire while the boys finished their chores. There weren't many chores to do. They didn't do much farming in the James family, although they had a good piece of arable land attached to the place. A couple of cornfields and a kitchen garden, hogs and chickens and two cows—that was the extent of their husbandry.

In the sitting room, they had a lynx and a grouse and woodpecker, all stuffed at home. And Mrs. James said with pride that Jim-Jim had done the stuffing. He had his own ideas about taxidermy, and they were original. The lynx in particular struck Judge Sheffield's fancy. It looked as if it were lying down on one elbow, stroking its chin, trying to decide whether or not to eat you up. But Judge Sheffield praised it and the spread-winged woodpecker, too.

Supper was sizzling all over the stove before Jim-Jim put in an appearance. They heard the baying of a couple of hounds far up the Chicken River, and later the rickety porch trembled under Jim-Jim's boots. The Judge had expected him to be big, maybe as big as Anson Heffelman, but he was nowhere near that size. He was skinny and wiry, and he had that same fierce Welsh face his mother had, with the brows and all.

The widow introduced Jim-Jim to Judge Sheffield. Jim-Jim wasn't one to make great speeches. He simply said that they were honored, and his little old mother beamed fondly upon him.

Fried chicken, pork, gravy, biscuits, hominy and potatoes, cabbage salad, layer cake, and two leftover pies. That was what they ate, together with liberal coffee and more kinds of pickle than ever hung upon a vine. Judge Sheffield began to be almost glad that Old Dick had become untied that afternoon.

"But won't your folks be worrying, Judge?" said Mrs. James, passing him his third helping of chicken.

"No, they won't," said the Judge. "There's just my sister, and she's used to having Dick traipse in. He comes home frequently that way. She'll just think I stopped at my nephew's place out on the Diamond Hill Road, and she'll never worry a whit."

"I wonder," said the youngest boy, "who could have untied him?"

Jim-Jim put down his fork and stared across the table with his queer, shining eyes. "Untied?"

"Certainly," said Sheffield. "I had him tied with a

halter—hitch and an extra half hitch beside. If Dick untied himself, he's more adept with his hoofs than I think he is. Human hands did that."

"Where was he tied?"

"Just across the river."

Jim-Jim said, kind of pondering, "That's the road toward the Heffelman place."

Judge Sheffield jumped, for as we know he had his suspicions.

The two younger boys said in chorus, "Anson Heffelman!" It rather sounded as if they were saying "Tweed Ring" or "Yellow Fever" or something like that.

"Of course," Old Judge Sheffield soothed them, "we don't really know that Anson Heffelman did it."

"I do," said Jim-Jim, breaking the silence in which he usually sat. "If a trap is sprung with a stick, it's Anse Heffelman that did it. If our Shep comes home weeping with a dose of pepper and salt in his hide, and he has done that, you can bank on Anse Heffelman. There are other things that have happened here, and I only hope they don't keep on happening, or I'm going to sample Anse Heffelman with a piece of .25-20 lead."

His mother shook her head. She looked grave and frightened. "Now, Jim-Jim."

"Just a weentsie sample," said Jim-Jim.

And the next boy muttered something about plugging a watermelon.

"Sure," agreed Jim-Jim. "A .25-20 doesn't make a big hole."

Judge Sheffield looked at them all severely. "I don't like such talk, my boys."

After that rebuke they were silent for a while. Mrs. James looked at the Judge with appreciation. You could see that she was thankful to have this admonishment spoken. It was hard for any woman, even a middle-aged one, to raise three wild-tempered boys, whose father was gone.

Woodsmen they were, and woodsmen they always had been, not farmers. Judge Sheffield got the story while Mrs. James washed the dishes and the youngest helped her kindly and Jim-Jim sat cleaning his rifle. Three years earlier they had come from Indiana, southern Indiana, which they called "Knobs," and no one of the Jameses was ever any fancy hand at farming. The boys liked to pretend among themselves that they were relatives of Jesse James, but there was no just cause for such claim.

It was growing late. The widow had to speak to Jim-Jim about hitching up the horse and wagon and driving Judge Sheffield into town.

"Not just yet, Ma," Jim-Jim pleaded. "Judge Sheffield doesn't want to go yet, do you, Judge?"

Sheffield sat back and smiled. "Well, I guess I did say my sister wouldn't worry."

The widow declared, "It's as good as settled. You can sleep in the little back bedroom, and heaven knows when we've been honored with a guest. I guess," she added a bit bashfully, "that you'll have to lay slantwise, the bed's so short. But you'll be warm as toast, for I'll give you the Log Cabin."

Jim-Jim and the boys began to clamor. "Not the Log Cabin. No, no," said young George. "The Bluebird, Ma!"

"Give him Jacob's Ladder," said little John. "I guess that's the warmest."

But Jim-Jim just smiled, as if he knew best, and shook his head. "The Blazing Star," he said, and his mother nodded.

"Of course," she murmured, "there's the Rose of Sharon."

"Of course," agreed Jim-Jim haughtily, "and there's the Wedding Ring and the Lock and Key and the Morning Glory, too. But I think he'll like the Blazing Star!"

Well you might believe that Judge Sheffield's jaw was hanging down. Just what they intended to offer him he didn't exactly know. Log cabins, ladders, rings, locks and keys, and such rubbish—it didn't sound as if he were going to rest in entire comfort.

The boys raced into the tiny front parlor, and then ensued a tremendous banging and bumping and clatter. Out they came, the three of them, each dragging a round-topped trunk. And Mrs. James stood and looked proud and rolled her crooked hands in her apron. The straps were unbuckled, the lids thrown back. Then Judge Sheffield understood.

Those three trunks were filled with quilts. And he said they were the loveliest quilts human eyes ever rested upon. Pink, cream, snow, blue, yellow, there was every kind of quilt that clever makers could devise and many that the Judge had never seen before. He began to think that Mrs. James was running a quilt factory, and he marveled when he heard she had worked all of these by her very own self.

"I never saw so many handsome quilts in my life," exclaimed the Judge, and then he persuaded her to tell him about them.

Meanwhile, the boys unfolded one after another, and their brown faces were excited. They acted as a bunch of young girls might have acted over an equal treasure. The Judge blinked. This was a race of hunters and woodsmen. These boys, he knew, spent their winters trapping and wading the cold snows, and their ancestors had before them. But they took a fervent pride in the soft and delicate stitchings of the calico folds.

"It was my grandmother started me," said Mrs. James in her mild and humble voice. "She was a great one for seaming and quilting, and even when her eyes went back on her, she could still do it, because of the sense that lay in her fingers. I used to sit by her when I was very small and thread the needles that her old eyes couldn't see to thread. That Fishtail, the one John's holding up, that brown-and-white Fishtail was the first I ever pieced, my own self. I've kept on making them through all my life. We've got everyday ones, crazy quilts, that we use on our beds now. But the boys won't let me use these except for special occasions, and their father never would before them."

"I don't wonder," gasped Judge Sheffield, and he stroked the Blazing Star, which Jim-Jim had spread across his gaunt knee. It started with flame and pink in the center of every huge exploding pattern. The little diamond-shaped pieces turned on through orange into yellow and then green and lilac, and finally they blazed again all around the edges. And the lines of quilting themselves, the painstaking stitches, the millions and millions of little thread dots in the whole rainbow expanse— they were a miracle to see.

"You did all this yourself?"

The widow nodded, as if she were a trifle ashamed of having spent so much time. "Oh, I did it when the boys were little. When one of them had the croup, maybe, and I had to more or less sit up with him. And before that— well, I was a maiden lady for some time previous to my marriage to Mr. James. Though I worked hard daytimes, I had to do something with hands in the evening, too. So I made a lot of quilts, to cover my family when finally I had one."

She picked up a quilt in her awkward, calloused hands,

touching it as lightly as one might caress the petals of a flower. "Kerosene lamp and candlelight, too," she said, and she seemed to be speaking to herself then. "But my eyes are good; they always were. I can sew easy enough. Sometimes when conditions were hard, when hard times have come upon us, I have been tempted to sell my quilts."

Judge Sheffield nodded. "I don't wonder. I calculate that they would bring ten dollars apiece from any store-keeper in Minnehaha."

Mrs. James fairly glowed with pleasure. "Oh, not that much, Judge Sheffield!"

"Yes, madam," he insisted. "Ten dollars is a good week's wages to many people, and certainly one of these is worth a week's wages."

The widow arose suddenly. Her face was still shining. "Come, boys. Put those back in the trunks now."

Judge Sheffield thought that she had indulged her pride beyond its common limits and dared do so no longer.

"Fold them careful and put them back in the trunk."

"But not the Blazing Star, Ma," said Jim-Jim.

And that night Judge Sheffield slept beneath it.

You might have thought that Judge Sheffield would have pursued his new friendship with the James family more closely. And indeed he would have, had it not been for law business and court business, which kept him oc-cupied through the last weeks of autumn and on through the first snowfalls. Often he planned to visit the Jameses, but he never seemed to find a free afternoon to allow Old Dick to take him out that way.

His next acquaintance with any member of the family came unexpectedly and with tragic surprise, on a cold day of early December, when the Judge heard a rush of snow-covered boots along the wooden platform outside his office.

He saw two bobsleds drawn up near the hitch rail. From the first sled men dragged out the weight of Anson Heffelman, pale faced, wound in blankets, but still able to swear between his blue lips. And a few moments afterward, from the second sled, two deputy sheriffs escorted Jim-Jim James, with his hands tied in front of him.

Old man Heffelman, Anson's father, was beside himself —waving a shotgun and calling the whole county to witness what he should do to Jim-Jim, who, he said, had shot down young Anse in cold blood and with malice aforethought.

That big bully of an Anse Heffelman was not nearly dead yet. They lugged him into Doc Ottway's office, and the mighty fellow fainted, in all his weakness, when he was brought near the warm stove. Doc Ottway probed for the bullet. It was a .25-20, all right, and lodged under Heffelman's shoulder blade. A few inches farther down, and they wouldn't have needed a doctor to do any probing.

Meanwhile, Jim-Jim was being blamed and badgered and threatened in the courthouse. His mother and the two young boys came driving into town soon afterward, but they weren't allowed to do more than speak a kind word to Jim-Jim. He was a felon now, charged with "assault with intent to kill." Preparations were made to bind him over to the grand jury.

Anse Heffelman's story went one way, when he was able to talk, and the James boy's story went another. Heffelman said that Jim-Jim had threatened him at various times, and on this day he was walking through the brush near his father's farm, not harming a soul or thinking any but the kindest thoughts, when Jim-Jim, carrying some furs, stepped from behind a tree and fired at him.

Jim-Jim, on the other hand, swore that he had been missing fur out of his traps. Trap after trap had been sprung, especially along the river next to the Heffelman farm, deadfalls and steel traps alike. There were signs of blood and fuzz, the marks of animals that had been caught.

Previously the James boys had built up a respectable fur trade. That was how they made most of their living. They caught muskrats, mink, weasels, foxes, and other creatures and shipped the fur to a well-known trading house, the Lefty Larsen Company of Minneapolis. Thus the missing fur represented a loss of income for the Jameses, and it was a serious situation with them.

This day the man tracks near the plundered traps were fresh in new-fallen snow. James James set out to follow them. He came out of the timber into the Heffelman's western cornfield, and there he saw young Anse striding through the stubble with a dead mink and a coon and a fox all swung over his shoulder.

Jim-Jim yelled, "You put down my fur!"

Anson told him to get off of Heffelman land.

Jim-Jim couldn't remember aiming or firing. When he came to himself, the sound of his rifle was echoing across the field and big Anse was howling in the snow. The Heffelman tribe came running at the shot, but they called a lot of neighbors before they essayed to take Jim-Jim into custody. The Heffelmans were a numerous, but not a courageous clan.

The thing that made Judge Sheffield feel most sorrowful was the thought that James James had certainly committed this deed in cold blood and with malice aforethought. The Judge himself had overheard a threat made by Jim-Jim, though naturally the Judge wasn't planning to mention it unless he were called upon to do so.

There were some political wires dangling in Minnehaha—trailing out of the county's political machinery, so to speak. Judge Sheffield couldn't refrain from pulling some of them. One thing—and that was good, since matters would soon get down to Jim-Jim's words against Anse Heffelman's—they reduced the charge of "assault with intent to kill." It was changed to "assault with intent to commit great bodily harm." The authorities were persuaded that no one could ever prove that Jim-Jim really wanted to do any killing.

Bail was placed at a thousand dollars. When the legal machinery had ceased its preliminary creaking, Jim-Jim found himself in the county jail, with nothing but brick walls and an unhappy, broken-legged stove for company. His mother left the younger boys in their old homemade sled and came and lamented in the snow outside the jail window.

Judge Sheffield swore that the whole thing gave him a terrible turn. He might have been able to scrape up the bail himself, although he was far from being a rich man, but he knew that public opinion wouldn't stand for that. The Heffelmans were politically active and politically venomous; they would have managed to have Judge Sheffield removed from the bench if he won their disfavor. The Judge reasoned correctly that he might better serve the needs of people like the Jameses if he remained in office.

"Jim-Jim," said Mrs. James, standing in the snow in her worn-out shoes, "you'll have to bear up for the next seven weeks. They say your trial won't come up till late in January. It would take a thousand dollars to release you."

Jim-Jim couldn't reply. His face was set and greenish pale; his hands twitched at the bars as if he hoped to tear them apart. Deadfalls were kinder than jail to a trapper like Jim-Jim, although certainly steel traps were not. It seemed to Judge Sheffield that this was rather a judgment of Nature—a steel trap catching and holding a wild creature, who, primitive and single-minded as any bobcat, had captured and held so many other things scarcely wilder than he.

That was on Friday, when it happened. On Monday town talk recited how Mrs. James was trying to mortgage her farm to win bail money for Jim-Jim. But her place wasn't worth much, and times were extremely hard that year. There was little livestock on the farm; the buildings and improvements were of the crudest sort. Eight hundred dollars was the most that any moneylender would offer her, and even then she had to beg and persuade, which doubtless pleased the Heffelmans no end.

Late that evening Judge Sheffield walked slowly homeward. He looked into the dark hulk of the little jail, and he shook his head. It was cold in there, and lonely; the jail fare wasn't of the best, though privately and secretly the Judge had done what he could to improve Jim-Jim's condition.

But when he reached his house, he was surprised to see a little box sled and an old thin horse before the door. The horse was blanketed against the frost. In the sitting room waited the Judge's old-maid sister and—he looked again—Mrs. Widow James. She sat stiff and straight on the platform rocker, still holding her shawls and knitted tippets around her, for she claimed she was too distraught to remove them.

Heaped over the carpet, hanging on chairs, bulking large across the table were her treasures: the quilts that

Judge Sheffield had seen drawn proudly out of their trunks the autumn before. Blazing Star, pink-and-tan Log Cabin, bold, bright Bluebird, the green-and-cream-colored Lock and Key—they were all there.

The widow shivered her hands and worked her shrunken little jaw. It was some time before she could speak.

"They're all here, Judge," she said. "All I have, except the crazy quilts, and I'm sure those wouldn't fetch much. But here are twenty. I recall you said that they ought to bring ten dollars apiece. I don't mind seeing them go, if they'll help to get Jim-Jim out of jail until his trial time. I've mortgaged the farm and raised eight hundred dollars that way."

The Judge could only stand there and gaze at the smooth, quilted beauties.

"Ten dollars apiece," said Mrs. James. "Maybe they ain't really worth it. But I recall you estimated that. Oh, it was just needle and thread, and more needles and thread, and old pieces of leftover dress goods, and a few ends of bolts that I bought special. A lot of these quilts are pretty old, so maybe they're not worth that much." She stood up and swallowed bravely. "That would add up to make the thousand dollars," she said. "The thousand dollars for Jim-Jim. If you know just where the two hundred dollars for the quilts could be had."

Judge Sheffield said afterward that he had more trouble managing his voice than the Widow James had managing hers. "I'll find the two hundred dollars," he said. "It will be simple as skat. Don't you worry any longer about Jim-Jim's bail. We'll have him out of there tomorrow morning."

Mrs. James dug down in her reticule and brought out her roll of greenbacks, squeezed from mortgaging the farm, and before ten o'clock the next forenoon Jim-Jim was temporarily freed from jail and hurrying through the white countryside to join his mother and brothers.

That was on December 11, when Jim-Jim left the discomfort of the jail behind him. I don't know what kind of Christmas and New Year's season the Jameses enjoyed, for Judge Sheffield's story used to skip over the time that elapsed until January 19. That was the day word reached town that Jim-Jim had disappeared.

The trial was due to begin on January 26, and Judge Sheffield was terribly concerned about it. He hadn't wanted to try Jim-Jim himself. He thought he had things managed nicely regarding the bar docket, and Jim-Jim would be tried during the time when old Judge Pettingill was sitting. Judge Sheffield couldn't trust himself. He had always administered justice fairly and wished to continue doing so. But he knew that his instincts would lead him to contrive an unconditional acquittal for Jim-Jim if it were a possible thing.

And that would not have been justice in its righteous and legal sense. After all, the shooting was a violation of the law. Judge Sheffield scratched his thin gray hair and thanked the Lord for old Judge Pettingill. He needn't have bothered, really. It appeared that the Lord loved Judge Pettingill so well that He gathered him unto Himself some three weeks after Christmas, with the aid of apple brandy, pork pie, overindulgence, and an outraged stomach. It happened that Judge Sheffield was the only judge available to try the cases coming up at that term of court. He scratched his hair even harder.

Then came the news of Jim-Jim's vanishment. The sheriff went out to talk to Mrs. James and the other boys.

"They don't know, or at least they claim they don't

know, anything about Jim-Jim," said the sheriff on his return. "And you ought to hear the Heffelmans howl about how the bail was placed too low! The Jameses just insist that Jim-Jim started before dawn, day before yesterday, to look at his trapline, and that he didn't come back. The younger boys found some furs and the rifle hanging in a tree on Glencoe Creek, but Jim-Jim's snowshoes had made tracks for the prairie."

Judge Sheffield chewed his penholder. "Do they seem worried?"

"Not precisely. I can't hardly tell. They seem to think the boy's able to take care of himself in the woods or on the prairie, though the mother swears she didn't advise him to run away and that he never mentioned planning to do so."

It wasn't his two hundred dollars that Judge Sheffield minded so much—that was about all the ready cash he had in the world, too. The important thing was that Jim-Jim had elected to become a fugitive from justice. Important and sad.

"Seven days to go," murmured Sheffield, and he prayed that Jim-Jim would return.

The Judge said that when he was at home he used to go in and look at the neat, folded quilts piled high on the spare bed downstairs. He'd finger them admiringly and touch them as if he expected foolishly to work mysterious magic and compel Jim-Jim to rise before him as the genie rose when Aladdin stroked the lamp. But the genie was a lot more accommodating than Jim-Jim.

No, the Judge couldn't sleep much, the night of January 25. When he appeared at the courthouse the next morning, there was a terrible rumpus going on. People were gossiping and quarreling and saying bitter things about Jim-Jim. Old Man Heffelman appeared, squalling about how he had been cheated out of justice and telling lugubriously that poor young Anse was still suffering so grievously that he wouldn't be able to appear until he was called as a witness.

Then came Mrs. James, with young George and John pale faced beside her. She whispered, when she could get Judge Sheffield's ear, that she would be willing to stand trial in Jim-Jim's stead. The Judge smiled sadly and patted her seamed hand.

"That can't be, Mrs. James," he declared. "But I do feel that Jim-Jim has done a cowardly thing in his failure to face the music."

Court had not been convened officially yet, for the county attorney and the lawyers and bailiffs and everybody else wrangled loudly about whether there was any use in picking a jury when the prisoner couldn't be produced. Judge Sheffield sat aloof behind his desk, trying not to look at Mrs. James and her two thin-faced sons, as they stared from a far corner of the courtroom.

There was a thunder of boots on the stairs. Men bellowed, "He's here! Here he comes! We've got the prisoner!"

James James it was, but he had a growth of beard on his face, and one of his boots was broken open and tied around with filthy, frozen rags. A deputy sheriff hauled him up to the bar. After Judge Sheffield had split his gavel and threatened everybody with contempt of court, he managed to achieve silence—a silence broken only by the queer little sound that Mrs. James made now and then when she gazed at Jim-Jim.

"I figured to get back by last night," Jim-Jim muttered in explanation. "I'm terribly sorry to have been delayed by a snowstorm in the line, and I hope I haven't committed any extra crime. But it's a dreadful long way to Minneapolis and—"

Judge Sheffield exploded. "Minneapolis! How on earth did you ever reach Minneapolis?"

"I walked, sir."

"But why did—"

"It was the quilts, Judge. Ma's quilts! I couldn't bear that she should lose them. They might not seem like much to some people, but to us Jameses. . . . And then, when I went out on my trapline that early morning, and there it was—dead under the deadfall—it seemed like it was a heavenly gift. I couldn't wait. I just had to light out and go, Judge. I had to!"

"Go?" the Judge demanded. "Go where, and with what?"

Jim-Jim said, "To Minneapolis. With that silver-tipped fox. I knew all along that there was one in the region, for I had seen him twice. And the Lefty Larsen Company had promised me two hundred dollars if the fur was prime. I was afraid to trust to shipment. My brothers were too young to send."

Well, that was it. He had caught a silver fox underneath one of his deadfall traps, and he had lugged that fox through days of tramping in the snow all the way to Minneapolis. Now he had the two hundred dollars, all folded up in a little dirty envelope, and he shoved it up on the desk into Judge Sheffield's hands.

"But, boy alive!" the Judge gasped. "This wasn't necessary. You were out on bail. It had been arranged."

"It was Ma's quilts," said Jim-Jim. "If we'd had anything else fit to sell, I wouldn't have cared. But can't she have them back now—the quilts—as long as the silver fox brought two hundred dollars? I'm eager to have you start along with my trial, though men told me on the stairs that Anse Heffelman isn't here to testify against me."

Old Man Heffelman brayed out, "He'll be here, all right! Just as soon as it's time for him to talk."

And from his seat on the clerk's desk nearby, big fat Doctor Ottway rolled his eyes. "I doubt it," he said distinctly.

Everybody looked at him, astonished.

"What do you mean?" demanded Mr. Heffelman. "You doubt it?"

Ottway smiled and looked mysteriously wise, as doctors do sometimes. "Just doubt it. That's all. I've got a little paper in my pocket that doubts it, too."

Judge Sheffield knit his brows and flashed some fire from his eyes, for his nerves had had about all they could stand. "If you've got anything to disclose, Ahab Ottway, disclose it right now. We'll see if we can save the state some money."

Thus enjoined, Doctor Ottway reluctantly produced his paper, though he had been planning to have himself called as a witness and create a sensation during the trial. It seems that young Heffelman got scared and feverish and thought he was going to die, that first night after he was shot. He worried about meeting the Lord's judgment, and he babbled and talked, and finally he made a full confession about stealing the fur and doing other annoyances to the Jameses. Doctor Ottway made him sign the confession. That's the reason young Anse pretended to be too sick to come to court on this day, though he didn't have the nerve to explain to his father.

Judge Sheffield said that it was all as plain as the nose on your face. He went into hurried consultation with the State. Then they produced the intelligence that such a shooting was a justifiable act, for any citizen had a right to defend his own personal property against robbers, and they quoted the State *vs.* Monahan, 1866, and the State *vs.* Schultz, 1871, as proof.

There were many things about the situation that couldn't occur now, when there are silver-fox farms here and there, and when two hundred dollars aren't running loose in the woods on four legs anymore. Courts and legal machinery are streamlined and formalized. Doubtless in this day and age a man like our good Doctor Ottway would be prosecuted for withholding such information in the hope of making his courtroom sensation and maybe winning new patients thereby.

And people nowadays would know more about the processes of law and bail, for it was explained honestly by those Jameses that they believed the bail money was all gone up Salt Creek. They thought they would never see it again—mortgaged farm, twenty quilts, and all. They thought, in simple words, that they had to pay a thousand dollars to get Jim-Jim out of jail until the time of his trial, and poor Jim-Jim believed it, too.

They were primitive people and knew more about turkeys and mink than they knew about courtrooms. Still, I hope that there are many of that breed left in America today.

So at last Judge Sheffield went home, to find the mound of quilts disappeared from his spare bedroom, carried happily away by Mrs. James and her boys in their sled. All but one, and that was the best and brightest quilt, the Blazing Star. They had left it as a sign of their love for Judge Sheffield. He used it always. It was over him when he died.

THE
KILLER
OF
HOURGLASS
LAKE

Robert Murphy

■

■■■

Halfway across the Hudson's Bay Company store Jerry Conrad conceived the notion that the box of .30-06 ammunition he had just bought should indicate to him, like the oracles of old, whether or not he was going to be lucky with the moose. It amused him that he should have such a notion, because he was rather scornful of oracles, superstitions, and, more than either, luck, which he claimed was a matter of preparation and attention to detail. He still held this point of view after being a bush pilot for a year, since graduating from college; he had been bush flying because he wanted some of the hunting and fishing of the country and because he wanted some actual flying in primitive country before going to work for his father's far-flung airline.

He began to toss the box from one hand to the other, thinking that if he could keep it in the air until he made the street and passed the little Anglican mission, he would know what the outcome of his trip was going to be.

He reached the screen door, turned and shoved it open with his back, eased himself through and carefully went down the steps. The street, which was a street by courtesy only, was rough and uneven, and he almost fell over a sleeping Indian dog before he saw it, but he managed to keep the box airborne. He was within ten yards of his goal when a voice called his name. He jumped, dropped the box, caught it on the toe of his moccasin, and almost kicked it up again, but it caromed off the side of the toe and fell to the ground. He picked it up and turned to see that good, graying man, Corporal Anderson, R.C.M.P., grinning at him.

"That was no time to interrupt a man," he said, grinning back. "Anybody else would say now that you cost him a moose."

"I didn't know you had one," Anderson said. There was just a shadow of a burr in his voice.

"I haven't got him yet," Jerry said. "If I'd got the box past the mission, it would have meant good luck. You prevented that, so I'm going to show you that I'll get him anyhow. I'm glad it was you, because you're always talking about luck."

Anderson's face got a little longer. "Don't talk like that, laddie," he said quickly, "especially after you've set up the test yourself. Don't go today: Wait a bit." He saw that Jerry was laughing at him, and shook his head. "You're too cocky for your own good. Was it a big one?"

"The biggest I've seen in—in many a long day."

The expression seemed a little unusual to the corporal. "Many a long day?" he asked.

"I read it in a book somewhere."

"I forgot you read books," Anderson said. "Where was this moose?"

"I won't tell you exactly," Jerry said. "But about three weeks ago I was flying back after delivering some stuff to Latour's trapping cabin and got off my course. I went over this lake. I'd never seen it before; it was shaped like an hourglass, with a long narrow arm off one side, and I saw him. I went down for a better look. He'll be a record for this country, so I thought I'd get in early."

"I don't know that lake," Anderson said. "I think you'd better give the location of it."

"You're still thinking about the box," Jerry teased him. "No, I'm not going to tell you. You'd be there getting in my way, just to keep the hoodoo off me. I'm surprised at a Calvinist like you talking in this fashion."

Anderson flushed slightly, and then grinned. "I can't very well hold with the powers of darkness," he said. "But I'm a bit older than you, and I've seen some odd things happen. I've decided it's best to speak softly of luck in a country as wild as this, where a man's alone so much. And there's another thing, Jerry. Some skulpie has been flying around shooting moose all over the place and just leaving them there. He's either crazy or after the biggest head in Canada, and he hasn't found it yet. We can control the kill by issuing licenses to sporting fellows like you who only want one moose, but this man is cleaning out the province. He'll exterminate our moose if we don't stop him."

"Nobody's seen him?" Jerry asked.

Anderson shook his head. "A couple of Indians say they've heard a plane. He apparently flies around early mornings and late afternoons, and stays quiet somewhere the rest of the day. But what I wanted to say is, don't interfere with him if you happen on him. Stay clear. Stand off and let me know. He's killed so much that we'll have to prosecute to the full extent and disgrace him, if only for the example, and he knows that. He may go to any length to avoid getting caught, even to killing a man if he thinks he can get away with it. Many a game warden's been killed for less. So don't chance it, laddie. He may get very rough."

"He may at that," Jerry said. "He certainly can't afford to get caught. Well, I'll buzz you if I see anything." He turned away, took a step, and paused. "Don't you want to go along? You could take a couple of days off. This is a record head, and you might get a shot at it."

"Thanks," Anderson said, "but I guess not. I've had fun shooting moose when I was younger, but after I got shot at myself a couple of times, I lost my taste for dishing it out."

"Oh, come now," Jerry said, surprised. "That's the sort

of state of mind you read about. I'll wait for you to pack up."

"No, thanks, I'm cured."

"I don't think it would cure me."

"Maybe not, maybe not," Anderson said. He waved and turned away, and Jerry went on down to the bay, where the plane was resting on its pontoons beside the battered wharf. The canoe was already tied along the top of the starboard pontoon and everything else was aboard. He cast off and climbed into the cabin as the light breeze slowly took him out, then started the engine. He made a long check run downwind, came about, and took off. As he gained altitude the big empty country opened up ahead of him, great dark areas of spruce glinting with little lakes and brightened with patches of the fragile gold and crimson of turning autumn leaves.

Having little to do but hold to his bearing, Jerry thought for a while about Anderson. He liked and respected Anderson, but was somewhat amused by the recollection of his expression when he, Jerry, ribbed him about the box. Anderson, as he had said, believed in speaking softly of such matters, just in case; he had been more concerned, really, with the omen's threat of bad luck to Jerry than with the outlaw moose killer. The imponderable bothered him more than bad men who could really give him trouble, Jerry thought, and looked at his watch. He looked at it again, not sure that he had seen it correctly the first time, for he was eight minutes overdue and the lake wasn't in sight yet.

He felt a quick sense of irritation, because he didn't do things like that. Being off course the first time he had seen the lake, woolgathering in a country where checkpoints were few and carefully watched, he had been particularly careful in plotting his course away from the place. He swore beneath his breath, swung east for ten minutes, and raised two lakes. Neither of them meant anything to him, and he ran the east leg for a few minutes more and then swung south for a while. A fair run in that direction brought him nothing either. He had pretty well boxed the country, to no purpose; he began to think about all the old prospectors of legend who stumbled upon fabulous lodes, went out for supplies, and then could never find their way back again.

This thought amused him hardly at all and his irritation grew. He decided that he had made a stupid mistake in his plotting and had better go home and do it over again, rather than fly aimlessly around until he got lost. Accordingly, with a sour grin of anticipation for what Anderson would have to say, he swung west. Seventeen minutes later he was over the lake.

It popped up in its hourglass form, which had looked like an entirely different body of water until he was almost directly above it, and he stared at it with a faint feeling of disbelief. The two large sides, lying east and west, were almost cut into two lakes by the narrow, hilly waist; the northern shore was a long, high ridge and had probably shielded the lake from him when he passed it before, which he was sure he had done, on the other side, before he turned east. The long arm ran out of the eastern lake in a direction a little east of north, and he could see the two beaver houses near the eastern side of the waist; they were on a sort of shelf, water lilies were very thick there, and it was where he had seen the moose. It was the same lake; there was no doubt of that.

"Well," he said, "Anderson would say that I've been bewitched."

The fine feeling of anticipation with which he had started on the trip, and which had slowly leaked away as he wandered all over the sky, came back again. He made a couple of wide circles, just to enjoy looking at the lake, then put the plane down on the western side. When he was on the water, with the dark, unbroken ranks of spruces all around, he grinned and shook hands with himself and slowly taxied through the narrows. The long tongue of land that came down from the north and made the waist was high and precipitous on the western side; it dropped sharply to flat and marshy ground, covered with willows and brush, on the east. As he came past the point into the eastern lake he was near the thick growth of lilies and not very far from the two big beaver houses standing several hundred yards out from the shore. A beaver swimming near one of them slapped the water with his tail and submerged with a great splash, and Jerry saluted it with a raised hand. He was rather bemused by beavers and their works, for he had read one of Washington Irving's books several months before in which a man named Colter had escaped the Cheyennes by hiding in a beaver house.

He had only half believed the tale, and as he taxied past the houses he felt a revulsion at the idea of crouching in that dank, black, and doubtless fetid place under the mound of mud and sticks. He shook the feeling off and continued slowly on until he reached the end of the narrow arm, where he stopped the engine and dropped anchor.

The silence that settled down upon him was a lovely thing; it seemed to reach to the end of the world. He stood on one of the pontoons for a little while and listened to it, then unlashed the canoe, put it into the water, and took his gear ashore. He found a level place in a little opening in the trees. There was a fine smell of spruce warmed by the sun in the air. He inflated his air mattress, set up his camp, and went off to cut a supply of firewood. A Canada jay appeared, cocked a bright and hopeful eye at him, and followed him back to camp.

He threw the wood down, and, looking around, decided that he had never made a better camp. He filled his pipe, lit it, and sat down on the mattress. There was no need to rush things, he thought; he'd take it easy, paddle out after a while, and watch from a distance to see if the moose appeared near the point toward sundown. If it did, he would arrange to be close to the beaver houses at the right time on the following evening. If it didn't, he would have to do some calling, although it was just a little early for that and he didn't like to kill moose that way.

The point was to kill the moose, and he had no doubt that he would do so. His eye fell on the bright cardboard cartridge box lying near the frying pan, and he grinned. An hour later, when the sun was getting low, he paddled down to the end of the arm and sat watching the point through his glasses. It wasn't very long before the great dark beast came out of the willows and splashed into the lake to dive for lily roots, carrying the unbelievable palmated antlers as though they weighed nothing at all.

The box of cartridges intruded itself upon his thoughts again the following afternoon by not being there. For a moment, Jerry had a very queer feeling when he didn't see it, for without cartridges he couldn't shoot anything, and it had been the box originally which had indicated, in his little game with it at the store, that he was going to be unsuccessful. He began, frantically, to turn everything upside down, and at the end of fifteen minutes he found it under the firewood, where it had no reason to be. He was in a great rage with it, he didn't believe in such nonsense anyhow, and although it had made him late he decided to take a little more time and burn it up. He was fed up with the thing; he put ten shells in his pocket, the other ten in a stewpan, tore the box in pieces, and touched a match to it.

"Now," he said, as the box was reduced to ashes, "that should take care of you once and for all."

The feeling of irritation stayed with him as he loaded the rifle, put it in the canoe, and started paddling down the long arm, but he forgot it as the arm opened into the lake and the excitement began to build up in him. The point was hidden from him by the curve of the shore and would be until he came to the beaver houses. He wouldn't know whether the moose was there until he came about in range of it, and as he eased the canoe carefully along near the bank he began to shake a little.

The sun had dropped behind the high western face of the waist; he was in shadow, and it seemed very cold. In the flat calm the drops of water from the paddle suddenly sounded like a drum and he stopped lifting it.

He slid along like a ghost and came under the lee of the first beaver house. It was a sore temptation not to edge out and look around it, but he stayed on the shoreward side until he was under the loom of the second house. He came up to it, caught hold of a stick, and worked the canoe backward until he could see past the sloping side. The lake by the point was empty.

As he sat staring at the blank water there was suddenly a great splashing and blowing out of his view toward the shore, and ripples ran out into the lake. He knew in-stantly what it was; the moose was working the bottom closer to shore, surfacing occasionally for air. He would have to move out to get a shot at it. He waited until quiet fell again, softly took the canoe out for a distance, put the paddle down, and picked up the rifle.

He hadn't long to wait. The great head broke the surface, and, as it was a little beyond the point and in the sun, the magnificent antlers glittered with a nimbus of fire, refracted light from the water drops on them. The moose turned and moved closer to the shore, its shoulders and back coming into view. It was a thing of such wild power and beauty against the golden water and the dark spruces of the far shore that Jerry, slowly bringing the rifle up, checked it halfway at the queer stab of protest within himself.

He fought the feeling down and began to move the rifle again, and it was on that instant that his quiet world exploded in his face. A great flail beat the water as the burst of machine-gun bullets, aimed a little too high, ripped above the moose's back and hit the lake; the yammering of the gun echoed between the wooded shores, immediately followed by the sudden deeper roar of airplane engines as throttles were shoved forward. The moose plunged wildly for the bank, and the amphibian, beginning to pull out of its dive, appeared around the point and went into a climbing turn to get back again.

It had all happened so quickly that Jerry sat there not believing it, a little stunned by the noise that beat around him. His eyes followed the plane incredulously as it swung, and he had the equally incredulous thought that he knew it, knew the black and orange bands running diagonally the length of the wings. It was headed back now. It turned toward him, came on with great speed, and began to dive. He remembered Anderson's warning then. He threw up his arm instinctively, and the machine gun began again. The burst hit the canoe about six inches from his knees, cut it in half, and he was floundering in the water. As his head came above the surface he saw the plane begin another swing and knew they were coming back to make sure of him.

He also knew he couldn't make the shore; it was too far and they would be waiting for him when he got there. He looked around desperately and saw the beaver house; he immediately thought of Colter, knew it was either that or nothing, and started for it. Some instinctive impulse made him snatch off his moccasins and stuff them into his shirt, and, fortunately, he hadn't many clothes on. He swam on the surface as long as he dared, in a sort of crawling expectancy of another burst.

The house loomed up, and he took a deep breath and dived. Halfway around it he found an entrance, dark and dubious in the clear water, and after hanging in indecision before it for a second or two, he pulled himself in and began to claw his way through the passage. He just about cleared the sides; it was abysmally black, soft mud swirled around him, and once he stuck. His breath was going and he thought he was finished, but the horror of drowning imprisoned in that black tunnel gave him strength enough to tear his way through. He was so spent when his head came into the air inside the house that he didn't hear the two startled beavers scurry about and plunge through the other exit.

The entrance he had come through opened above the water line, onto a muddy floor; and as soon as he had recovered sufficiently, he squirmed a little farther out of the passage, got out his waterproof matchbox, and struck a light. The inside of the house was hemispherical, about six feet across and a little over two feet high, plastered with mud except around the top, where a little air found its way through the pile of mud and sticks above. The beavers had brought in grass and shredded wood fibers for their beds against the walls. It was muddy and dank and almost like being buried alive, but as his breath and equanimity returned he congratulated himself rather ruefully on the fact that it was better than being dead. A long-forgotten tag end of college poetry popped into his head:

Find out some uncouth cell,
Where brooding Darkness spreads his jealous wings. . .

and he wondered if Colter, who had discovered the utility of beaver houses, had ever read Milton. But he didn't dwell very long on that. He had to get out of the place after dark, and the memory of the moment when he had stuck fast coming in filled him with such horror that he knew he couldn't think of that either; he would have to forget that, blot it out of his mind, and face it when he came to it. He struck another match and looked at his watch, which, fortunately, was still running. It would be an hour or more before he could leave. He had no idea what his procedure would be when he got out; he didn't know what the people who thought they had murdered him would do, but he suspected that they would make a thorough job of his plane and gear. He was lucky in that it was early in a warm fall, but he knew he couldn't last long or walk out the two-hundred-odd miles or more with the few clothes he had on, no compass, and no food.

His situation wasn't good, but, as his teeth chattered in the dark, he decided it wasn't hopeless either. He was sure he could plan something. He thought again of the plane banking to come at him, the bands on the wings, and remembered now what he hadn't time to remember before; it belonged to Joe Dufore, another bush pilot, whom he knew and had never trusted very much. Hot and murderous rage took hold of him and slowly shifted to a cold determination to live long enough, somehow, to square things with that man. He sat shivering in the muddy dark, thinking of Dufore and the time when he would have to leave the beaver house; it would be the worst journey that he would ever make.

Nearly two hours later he stood on the shore near the point and saw the glow of the fire across the lake on the south shore. His first thought, of stealing in after they were asleep, was finished almost upon its inception by the sudden barking of a dog. It barked two or three times and was answered by a loon, and then silence fell again. Coming on top of everything else that had happened, it was the crowning frustration, but Jerry was so enured to trouble for that day that he merely shrugged as though he had been expecting it and turned away. He was very tired and very cold; the air had taken on a penetrating chill when the sun went down, and he had to have a fire.

He made his way up the long arm toward his camp, cut inland over a little ridge, and against a rock ledge on the downward slope built the fire, warmed himself, and dried his clothes. The waning moon gave enough light, so he went on to his campsite and found that everything was gone. Dufore had worked fast before dark, probably loading the plane with his gear and taking it out into deep water and sinking it; he cursed Dufore for that and went back to his fire under the ledge, sleeping for the rest of the night.

He was in the spruces above the point a little after

dawn and was surprised to see a canoe tied to the amphibian, which was moored several hundred yards off the end of the point. The canoe mystified him for a while, but at the end of half an hour's wait he saw Dufore get out of the plane and paddle across the lake to the south shore, where the fire had been the previous night. The dog barked again, and he knew then that Dufore was not alone, that he was working for someone else who stayed in the camp. Apparently Dufore slept in the plane, possibly to keep any wandering and curious Indians out of it, and a sudden wild hope took hold of him.

If only they didn't leave today, he thought, he might be able to do it. He watched anxiously for several hours, but they gave no indication of moving. Around noon Dufore paddled out and moved the plane around to the western side of the waist, and from that Jerry estimated that they were getting it out of the moose's view and had decided to stay a few more days to see if they could get another shot at the animal.

The day wore on without any further sign of life from them, and Jerry grew hungrier. The sun sank lower and the moose didn't appear, chiefly, Jerry reasoned, because it still remembered its fright and because his scent was all over the place. About dusk Dufore paddled out again and got into the plane. Jerry watched awhile and went back to the fire under the ledge.

He was back about two o'clock and slipped around the point in the pale moonlight until he could see the plane. Between the chill and his nervousness about how his enterprise was going to succeed, he was shaking badly, but after he got into the water and began to swim out, he grew calmer again. He reached the plane and eased himself around to the door. He had another fit of shakes there, for everything depended upon how Dufore would react, whether he could get the man to the door before he was fully awake. With great care, inch by inch, he got himself up on the bulge of the hull; the plane canted with his weight, and he heard the first sleepy grumble from inside.

He tapped on the window, calling out with low urgency, "Joe! Joe!"

He hoped that Dufore, half awake and startled, would come without thinking at the use of his name; it was what Dufore did. Dufore opened the door and saw, wan in the moonlight, the face of a man he thought dead. The sight paralyzed him for an instant; he gasped out, "Ah, Seigneur!" and Jerry hit him, full force, at the base of the skull with the edge of his hand. He put all he had into the blow: his hatred of the unknown man who was responsible for his trouble and whom he couldn't reach, and his hatred of Dufore for being with him. Dufore collapsed, and Jerry climbed into the cabin.

He got the limp Dufore back into the cargo space behind the seats, found enough rope to tie him up, and gagged him with a glove. Then he rooted around in the dim light until he found dry clothes and some food. It was mostly crackers and canned meat, but it tasted fine; he ate as much as he could hold and sat down to wait for Dufore to come to.

Dufore regained consciousness slowly and reluctantly, but Jerry had plenty of time. He got up and found a wrench and sat down beside the man again. When Dufore was ready, Jerry shook the wrench at him.

"Will you keep quiet if I take the gag out," he asked, "or will you yell and take a tap with this? I have a lot of reasons to be very enthusiastic with it."

Dufore shook his head, and Jerry took the gag out; a great spate of whispered words followed it. "Ah, *mon dieu,* I did not know he is going to shoot. He is surprised. We do not see you until we come past the point. He is very big man, to get caught is very bad for him. He goes crazy. Now he is very afraid. He watches me, the dog watches me. I—"

"Liar," Jerry said. "You were in it as deeply as he was, and well paid for it. All I want to know is whether you were taking off early in the morning. I've got to get close to him to make my run if the wind stays where it is."

"Yes, yes, we were to fly at dawn to look around. He is mad, this one. You let me loose, we fix—"

Jerry shoved the glove into his mouth again and left him. He took the line from the canoe and brought the end of it into the pilot's window. At the first streak of light he started the engines, let them warm up, and taxied through the narrows, towing the canoe. He made a wide swing around toward the camp, straightened away, dropped the canoe line, and shoved the throttles in. In the strengthening light he could see the figure of the man begin to run along the shore.

An hour later he managed to raise a ham operator on the radio. He gave the ham a synopsis of what had happened, asked him to report it to Anderson and tell Anderson that he was bringing Dufore in.

They were sitting in Anderson's office later that morning with cups of tea nearly as black as tar; Dufore had been stowed away, and Jerry had gone over his tale. Anderson sat behind his desk, puffing a cloud of pipe smoke occasionally and looking almost benign. He had already called for the police *Norseman* and said it was due late that afternoon.

"I'm not sure who the man is yet," he said, "but I suspect this will cause a stir in Montreal. I think I have

heard of the dog before. There is a rich head hunter. . . .
They were pretty clever about it, weren't they? Dufore
had reason to be many places all the time and as long as
they weren't seen together, no one would connect them.
The man I think of has a plane of his own, but of course
he never used it." He puffed on his pipe for a moment
and smiled. "What did you think of in the beaver house?"

"Dufore," Jerry said, "and whether I was going to be
able to face that passage again to get out."

"You didn't think about luck?" Anderson asked, with
all the appearance of innocence.

"Luck?" Jerry asked. "Now look—"

Anderson stopped him with a raised hand. "Perhaps,"
he said, "you read an obscure book once because you
planned to hide later in a beaver house. It was a wise
move." He smiled again. "It was also wise that you kept
them at your lake. The walk out is a long one."

"Now look," Jerry said again. "I could have probably
found the rifle again, if they'd left. Enough diving—"

"How deep was the water?"

"Pretty deep there," Jerry said, a little abashed. "I had
to get off the shelf the houses were on."

"Pretty deep," Anderson said, and another puff of pipe
smoke went up. "Well. But never mind that. The thing
that interests me, laddie, is the wee box. The cartridge
box. The box said you wouldn't kill the moose, and you
haven't killed him yet. You haven't proved it wrong. You
were interrupted. Now then. You can recover enough
from this man to buy a new plane and outfit, or I can
have you dropped at the lake all equipped tomorrow. For
as long as you want, for a conclusive test of whether the
box was right or not."

He had got a sort of pleased, sly expression, and his
half-closed eyes gleamed with humor.

Jerry thought a moment before he answered. "The devil fly off with you," he said finally. "I think you know what I'm going to say."

"Do I?" Anderson asked. "Do I now? Maybe you're going to tell me there might be such a thing as luck? Maybe you're going to let an old man win an argument?"

"I'm going to let you win by default," Jerry said, with a grin. "I'm not going back. I don't want to shoot that moose. Remember, I've been shot at, too, now. Like you, I've sort of lost my taste for dishing it out."

THE
MOST
DANGEROUS
GAME
Richard Connell

■ ■ ■

Off there to the right, somewhere, is a large island," said Whitney. "It's rather a mystery. . . ."

"What island is it?" Rainsford asked.

"The old charts call it Ship-Trap Island," Whitney replied. "A suggestive name, isn't it? Sailors have a curious dread of the place. I don't know why. Some superstition. . . ."

"Can't see it," remarked Rainsford, trying to peer through the dank tropical night that was palpable as it pressed its thick warm blackness in upon the yacht.

"You've good eyes," said Whitney, with a laugh, "and I've seen you pick off a moose moving in the brown fall brush at four hundred yards, but even you can't see four miles or so through a moonless Caribbean night."

"Nor four yards," admitted Rainsford. "Ugh! It's like moist velvet."

"It will be light enough in Rio," promised Whitney. "We should make it in a few days. I hope the jaguar guns have come from Purdey's. We should have some good hunting up the Amazon. Great sport, hunting."

"The best sport in the world," agreed Rainsford.

"For the hunter," amended Whitney. "Not for the jaguar."

"Don't talk rot, Whitney," said Rainsford. "You're a big-game hunter, not a philosopher. Who cares how a jaguar feels?"

"Perhaps the jaguar does," observed Whitney.

"Bah! They've no understanding."

"Even so, I rather think they understand one thing at least—fear. The fear of pain and the fear of death."

"Nonsense," laughed Rainsford. "This hot weather is making you soft, Whitney. Be a realist. The world is made up of two classes—the hunters and the hunted.

Luckily, you and I are hunters. Do you think we've passed that island yet?"

"I can't tell in the dark. I hope so."

"Why?" asked Rainsford.

"The place has a reputation—a bad one."

"Cannibals?" suggested Rainsford.

"Hardly. Even cannibals wouldn't live in such a god-forsaken place. But it's got into sailor lore somehow. Didn't you notice that the crew's nerves seem a bit jumpy today?"

"They were a bit strange, now you mention it. Even Captain Nielsen. . . ."

"Yes, even that tough-minded old Swede, who'd go up to the devil himself and ask him for a light. Those fishy blue eyes held a look I never saw there before. All I could get out of him was: 'This place has an evil name among seafaring men, sir.' Then he said to me, very gravely, 'Don't you feel anything?' as if the air about us was actually poisonous. Now you mustn't laugh when I tell you this—I did really feel something like a sudden chill.

"There was no breeze. The sea was as flat as a plate-glass window. We were drawing near the island then. What I felt was a—a mental chill—a sort of sudden dread."

"Pure imagination," said Rainsford. "One superstitious sailor can taint the whole ship's company with his fear."

"Maybe. But sometimes I think sailors have an extra sense that tells them when they are in danger. Sometimes I think evil is a tangible thing, with wave lengths, just as sound and light have. An evil place can, so to speak, broadcast vibrations of evil. Anyhow, I'm glad we're getting out of this zone. Well, I think I'll turn in now, Rainsford."

"I'm not sleepy," said Rainsford. "I'm going to smoke another pipe up on the afterdeck."

"Good night then, Rainsford. See you at breakfast."

"Right. Good night, Whitney."

There was no sound in the night as Rainsford sat there, but the muffled throb of the engine that drove the yacht swiftly through the darkness and the swish and ripple of the wash of the propeller.

Rainsford, reclining in a steamer chair, indolently puffed on his favorite briar. The sensuous drowsiness of the night was on him. It's so dark, he thought, that I could sleep without closing my eyes; the night would be my eyelids. . . .

An abrupt sound startled him. Off to the right he heard it, and his ears, expert in such matters, could not be mistaken. Again he heard the sound, and again. Somewhere, off in the blackness, someone had fired a gun three times.

Rainsford sprang up and moved quickly to the rail, mystified. He strained his eyes in the direction from which the reports had come, but it was like trying to see through a blanket. He leaped upon the rail and balanced himself there, to get a greater elevation; his pipe, striking a rope, was knocked from his mouth. He lunged for it; a short, hoarse cry came from his lips as he realized he had reached too far and had lost his balance. The cry was pinched off short as the blood-warm waters of the Caribbean Sea closed over his head.

He struggled up to the surface and tried to cry out, but the wash from the speeding yacht slapped him in the face and the saltwater in his open mouth made him gag and strangle. Desperately he struck out with strong strokes after the receding lights of the yacht, but he stopped before he had swum fifty feet. A certain cool headedness had come to him; it was not the first time he had been in a tight place. There was a chance that his cries would be heard by someone aboard the yacht, but that chance was slender and grew more slender as the yacht raced on. He wrestled himself out of his clothes and shouted with all his power. The lights of the yacht became faint and ever-vanishing fireflies; then they were blotted out entirely by the night.

Rainsford remembered the shots. They had come from the right, and doggedly he swam in that direction, swimming with slow, deliberate strokes, conserving his strength. For a seemingly endless time he fought the sea. He began to count his strokes desperately; he could do possibly a hundred more and then. . . .

Rainsford heard a sound. It came out of the darkness, a high, screaming sound, the sound of an animal in an extremity of anguish and terror. He did not recognize the animal that made the sound; he did not try to. With fresh vitality he swam toward the sound. He heard it again; then it was cut short by another noise, crisp, staccato.

"Pistol shot," muttered Rainsford, swimming on.

Ten minutes of determined effort brought another sound to his ears, the most welcome he had ever heard, the muttering and growling of the sea breaking on a rocky shore. He was almost on the rocks before he saw them; on a night less calm he would have been shattered against them. With his remaining strength he dragged himself from the swirling waters. Jagged crags appeared to jut up into the opaqueness; he forced himself upward, hand over hand. Gasping, his hands raw, he reached a flat place at the top. Dense jungle came down to the very edge of the cliffs. What perils that tangle of trees and underbrush might hold for him did not concern Rainsford just then. All he knew was that he was safe from his enemy, the sea, and that utter weariness was on him. He flung himself down at the jungle edge and tumbled headlong into the deepest sleep of his life.

When he opened his eyes he knew from the position of the sun that it was late in the afternoon. Sleep had given him new vigor; a sharp hunger was picking at him. He looked about him, almost cheerfully.

Where there are pistol shots, there are men. Where there are men, there is food, he thought. But what kind of men, he wondered, in so forbidding a place? An unbroken front of snarled and jagged jungle fringed the shore.

He saw no sign of a trail through the closely knit web of weeds and trees; it was easier to go along the shore, and Rainsford floundered along by the water. Not far from where he had landed, he stopped.

Some wounded thing, by the evidence a large animal, had thrashed about in the underbrush; the jungle weeds were crushed down and the moss was lacerated; one patch of weeds was stained crimson. A small, glittering object not far away caught Rainsford's eye, and he picked it up. It was an empty cartridge.

"A .22," he remarked. "That's odd. It must have been a fairly large animal, too. The hunter had his nerve to tackle it with a light gun. It's clear that the brute put up a fight. I suppose the hunter flushed his quarry and wounded it with the first three shots I heard. Then he trailed it here and finished it with the last."

He examined the ground closely and found what he had hoped to find—the print of hunting boots. They pointed along the cliff in the direction he had been going.

Eagerly he hurried along, now slipping on a rotten log or a loose stone, but making headway. Night was beginning to settle down on the island.

Bleak darkness was blacking out the sea and jungle when Rainsford sighted the lights. He came upon them as he turned a crook in the coastline, and his first thought was that he had come upon a village, for there were many lights. But as he forged along he saw to his great astonishment that all the lights were in one enormous building, a lofty structure with pointed towers plunging upward into the gloom. His eyes made out the shadowy outlines of a palatial chateau; it was set on a high bluff, and on three sides of it cliffs dived down to where the sea licked greedy lips in the shadows.

Mirage, thought Rainsford. But it was no mirage, he found, when he opened the tall, spiked iron gate. The stone steps were real enough; the massive door with a leering gargoyle for a knocker was real enough; yet about it all hung an air of unreality.

He lifted the knocker, and it creaked up stiffly, as if it had never before been used. He let it fall, and it startled him with its booming loudness. He thought he heard footsteps within; the door remained closed. Again Rainsford lifted the heavy knocker and let it fall. The door opened then, opened as suddenly as if it were on a spring, and Rainsford stood blinking in the river of gold light that poured out. The first thing Rainsford's eyes discerned was the largest man Rainsford had ever seen, a gigantic creature, solidly made and black bearded to the waist. In his hand the man held a long-barrel revolver, and he was pointing it straight at Rainsford's heart.

Out of the snarl of beard two small eyes regarded Rainsford.

"Don't be alarmed," said Rainsford, with a smile which he hoped was disarming. "I'm no robber. I fell off a yacht. My name is Sanger Rainsford of New York City."

The menacing look in the eyes did not change. The revolver pointed as rigidly as if the giant were a statue. He gave no sign that he understood Rainsford's words or that he had even heard them. He was dressed in uniform, a black uniform trimmed with gray astrakhan.

"I'm Sanger Rainsford of New York," Rainsford began again. "I fell off a yacht. I am hungry."

The man's only answer was to raise with his thumb the hammer of his revolver. Then Rainsford saw the man's free hand go to his forehead in a military salute, and he saw him click his heels together and stand at attention. Another man was coming down the broad marble steps, an erect, slender man in evening clothes. He advanced to Rainsford and held out his hand.

In a cultivated voice marked by a slight accent that gave it added precision and deliberateness, he said, "It is a very great pleasure and honor to welcome Mr. Sanger Rainsford, the celebrated hunter, to my home."

Automatically Rainsford shook the man's hand.

"I've read your book about hunting snow leopards in Tibet, you see," explained the man. "I am General Zaroff."

Rainsford's first impression was that the man was singularly handsome; his second was that there was an original, almost bizarre quality about the general's face. He was a tall man past middle age, for his hair was a vivid white, but his thick eyebrows and pointed military mustache were as black as the night from which Rainsford had come. His eyes, too, were black and very bright. He had high cheekbones, a sharp-cut nose, a spare, dark face, the face of a man used to giving orders, the face of an aristocrat. Turning to the giant in uniform, the general made a sign. The giant put away his pistol, saluted, withdrew.

"Ivan is an incredibly strong fellow," remarked the general, "but he has the misfortune to be deaf and dumb. A simple fellow, but, I'm afraid, like all his race, a bit of a savage."

"Is he Russian?"

"He is a Cossack," said the general, and his smile showed red lips and pointed teeth. "So am I."

"Come," he said, "we shouldn't be chatting here. We can talk later. Now you want clothes, food, rest. You shall have them. This is a most restful spot."

Ivan had reapppeared, and the general spoke to him with lips that moved but gave forth no sound.

"Follow Ivan, if you please, Mr. Rainsford," said the general. "I was about to have my dinner when you came. I'll wait for you. You'll find that my clothes will fit you, I think."

It was to a huge, beam-ceilinged bedroom with a canopied bed big enough for six men that Rainsford followed the silent giant. Ivan laid out an evening suit, and Rainsford, as he put it on, noticed that it came from a London tailor who ordinarily cut and sewed for none below the rank of duke.

The dining room to which Ivan conducted him was in many ways remarkable. There was a medieval magnificence about it; it suggested a baronial hall of feudal times with its oaken panels, its high ceiling, its vast refectory table where twoscore men could sit down to eat. About the hall were the mounted heads of many animals —lions, tigers, elephants, moose, bears; larger or more perfect specimens Rainsford had never seen. At the great table the general was sitting, alone.

"You'll have a cocktail, Mr. Rainsford," he suggested. The cocktail was surpassingly good, and, Rainsford noted, the table appointments were of the finest, the linen, the crystal, the silver, the china.

They were eating borsch, the rich, red soup with sour cream so dear to Russian palates. Half apologetically General Zaroff said, "We do our best to preserve the amenities of civilization here. Please forgive any lapses. We are well off the beaten track, you know. Do you think the champagne has suffered from its long ocean trip?"

"Not in the least," declared Rainsford. He was finding the general a most thoughtful and affable host, a true cosmopolite. But there was one small trait of the general's that made Rainsford uncomfortable. Whenever he looked up from his plate he found the general studying him, appraising him narrowly.

"Perhaps," said General Zaroff, "you were surprised that I recognized your name. You see, I read all books on hunting published in English, French, and Russian. I have but one passion in my life, Mr. Rainsford, and it is the hunt."

"You have some wonderful heads here," said Rainsford, as he ate a particularly well-cooked filet mignon. "That Cape buffalo is the largest I ever saw."

"Oh, that fellow. Yes, he was a monster."

"Did he charge you?"

"Hurled me against a tree," said the general. "Fractured my skull. But I got the brute."

"I've always thought," said Rainsford, "that the Cape buffalo is the most dangerous of all big game."

For a moment the general did not reply; he was smiling his curious red-lipped smile. Then he said slowly, "No. You are wrong, sir. The Cape buffalo is not the most dangerous big game." He sipped his wine. "Here in my preserve on this island," he said in the same slow tone, "I hunt more dangerous game."

Rainsford expressed his surprise. "Is there big game on this island?"

The general nodded. "The biggest."

"Really?"

"Oh, it isn't here naturally, of course. I have to stock the island."

"What have you imported, General?" Rainsford asked. "Tigers?"

The general smiled. "No," he said. "Hunting tigers ceased to interest me some years ago. I exhausted their possibilities, you see. No thrill left in tigers, no real danger. I live for danger, Mr. Rainsford."

The general took from his pocket a gold cigarette case and offered his guest a long black cigarette with a silver tip; it was perfumed and gave off a smell like incense.

"We will have some capital hunting, you and I," said the general. "I shall be most glad to have your society."

"But what game—" began Rainsford.

"I'll tell you," said the general. "You will be amused, I know. I think I may say, in all modesty, that I have done a rare thing. I have invented a new sensation. May I pour you another glass of port, Mr. Rainsford?"

"Thank you, General."

The general filled both glasses, and said, "God makes some men poets. Some he makes kings, some beggars. Me He made a hunter. My hand was made for the trigger, my father said. He was a very rich man with a quarter of a million acres in the Crimea, and he was an ardent sportsman. When I was only five years old he gave me a little gun, specially made in Moscow for me, to shoot sparrows with. When I shot some of his prize turkeys with it, he did not punish me; he complimented me on my marksmanship. I killed my first bear in the Caucasus when I was ten. My whole life has been one prolonged hunt. I went into the Army—it was expected of noblemen's sons—and for a time commanded a divison of Cossack cavalry, but my real interest was always the hunt. I have hunted every kind of game in every land. It would be impossible for me to tell you how many animals I have killed."

The general puffed at his cigarette. "After the debacle in Russia I left the country, for it was imprudent for an officer of the czar to stay there. Many noble Russians lost everything. I, luckily, had invested heavily in American securities, so I shall never have to open a tearoom in Monte Carlo or drive a taxi in Paris. Naturally, I continued to hunt—grizzlies in your Rockies, crocodiles in the Ganges, rhinoceroses in East Africa. It was in Africa that the Cape buffalo hit me and laid me up for six months. As soon as I recovered I started for the Amazon to hunt jaguars, for I had heard they were unusually cunning. They weren't."

The Cossack sighed. "They were no match at all for a hunter with his wits about him, and a high-powered rifle. I was bitterly disappointed. I was lying in my tent with a splitting headache one night when a terrible thought pushed its way into my mind. Hunting was beginning to bore me! And hunting, remember, had been my life. I have heard that in America businessmen often go to pieces when they give up the business that has been their life."

"Yes, that's so," said Rainsford.

The general smiled. "I had no wish to go to pieces," he said. "I must do something. Now, mine is an analytical mind, Mr. Rainsford. Doubtless that is why I enjoy the problems of the chase."

"No doubt, General Zaroff."

"So," continued the general, "I asked myself why the hunt no longer fascinated me. You are much younger than I am, Mr. Rainsford, and have not hunted as much, but you perhaps can guess the answer."

"What was it?"

"Simply this: hunting had ceased to be what you call 'a sporting proposition.' It had become too easy. I always got my quarry. Always. There is no greater bore than perfection."

The general lit a fresh cigarette. "No animal had a chance with me anymore. That is no boast; it is a mathematical certainty. The animal had nothing but his legs and his instinct. Instinct is no match for reason. When I thought of this it was a tragic moment for me, I can tell you."

Rainsford leaned across the table, absorbed in what his host was saying.

"It came to me as an inspiration what I must do," the general went on.

"And that was?"

The general smiled the quiet smile of one who has faced an obstacle and surmounted it with success. "I had to invent a new animal to hunt," he said.

"A new animal? You are joking."

"Not at all," said the general. "I never joke about hunting. I needed a new animal. I found one. So I bought this island, built this house, and here I do my hunting. The island is perfect for my purposes—there are jungles with a maze of trails in them, hills, swamps—"

"But the animal, General Zaroff?"

"Oh," said the general, "it supplies me with the most exciting hunting in the world. No other hunting compares with it for an instant. Every day I hunt, and I never grow bored now, for I have a quarry with which I can match my wits."

Rainsford's bewilderment showed in his face.

"I wanted the ideal animal to hunt," explained the general. "So I said: 'What are the attributes of an ideal quarry?' And the answer was, of course: 'It must have courage, cunning, and, above all, it must be able to reason.'"

"But no animal can reason," objected Rainsford.

"My dear fellow," said the general, "there is one that can."

"But you can't mean—" said Rainsford with a gasp.

"And why not?"

"I can't believe you are serious, General Zaroff. This is a grisly joke."

"Why should I not be serious? I am speaking of hunting."

"Hunting? Good God, General Zaroff, what you speak of is murder."

The general laughed with entire good nature. He regarded Rainsford quizzically. "I refuse to believe that so modern and civilized a young man as you seem to be harbors romantic ideas about the value of human life. Surely your experiences in the war. . . ." He stopped.

"Did not make me condone cold-blooded murder," finished Rainsford stiffly.

Laughter shook the general. "How extraordinarily droll you are!" he said. "One does not expect nowadays to find a young man of the educated class, even in America, with such a naïve, and, if I may say so, mid-Victorian point of view. It's like finding a snuffbox in a limousine. Ah, well, doubtless you had Puritan ancestors. So many Americans appear to have had. I'll wager you'll forget your notions when you go hunting with me. You've a genuine new thrill in store for you, Mr. Rainsford."

"Thank you, I'm a hunter, not a murderer."

"Dear me," said the general, quite unruffled, "again that unpleasant word. But I think I can show you that your scruples are quite ill founded."

"Yes?"

"Life is for the strong, to be lived by the strong, and, if needs be, taken by the strong. The weak of the world were put here to give the strong pleasure. I am strong. Why should I not use my gift? If I wish to hunt, why should I not? I hunt the scum of the earth—sailors from tramp ships, lascars, blacks, Chinese, whites, mongrels— a thoroughbred horse or hound is worth more than a score of them."

"But they are men," said Rainsford hotly.

"Precisely," said the general. "That is why I use them. It gives me pleasure. They can reason, after a fashion. So they are dangerous."

The general's left eyelid fluttered down in a wink. "This island is called Ship Trap," he answered. "Sometimes an angry god of the high seas sends them to me. Sometimes, when Providence is not so kind, I help Providence a bit. Come to the window with me."

Rainsford went to the window and looked out toward the sea.

"Watch! Out there!" exclaimed the general, pointing into the night. Rainsford's eyes saw only blackness, and then, as the general pressed a button, far out to sea Rainsford saw the flash of lights.

The general chuckled. "They indicate a channel," he said "where there's none: giant rocks with razor edges crouch like a sea monster with wide-open jaws. They can crush a ship as easily as I crush this nut." He dropped a walnut on the hardwood floor and brought his heel grinding down on it. "Oh, yes," he said casually, as if in answer to a question, "I have electricity. We try to be civilized here."

"Civilized? And you shoot down men?"

A trace of anger was in the general's black eyes, but it was there for but a second, and he said, in his most pleasant manner, "Dear me, what a righteous young man you are! I assure you I do not do the thing you suggest. That would be barbarous. I treat these visitors with every consideration. They get plenty of good food and exercise. They get into splendid physical condition. You shall see for yourself tomorrow."

"What do you mean?"

"We'll visit my training school." The general smiled. "It's in the cellar. I have about a dozen pupils down there now. They're from the Spanish bark *San Lucar* that had the bad luck to go on the rocks out there. A very inferior lot, I regret to say. Poor specimens and more accustomed to the deck than to the jungle."

He raised his hand, and Ivan, who served as waiter, brought thick black coffee. Rainsford, with an effort, held his tongue in check.

"It's a game, you see," pursued the general blandly. "I suggest to one of them that we go hunting. I give him a supply of food and an excellent hunting knife. I give him three hours' start. I am to follow, armed only with a pistol of the smallest caliber and range. If my quarry eludes me for three whole days, he wins the game. If I find him"—the general smiled—"he loses."

"Suppose he refuses to be hunted."

"Oh," said the general, "I give him his option, of

course. He need not play that game if he doesn't wish to. If he does not wish to hunt, I turn him over to Ivan. Ivan once had the honor of serving as official knouter to the Great White Czar, and he has his own ideas of sport. Invariably, Mr. Rainsford, invariably they choose the hunt."

"And if they win?"

The smile on the general's face widened. "To date I have not lost," he said.

Then he added, hastily, "I don't wish you to think me a braggart, Mr. Rainsford. Many of them afford only the most elementary sort of problem. Occasionally I strike a tartar. One almost did win. I eventually had to use the dogs."

"The dogs?"

"This way, please. I'll show you."

The general steered Rainsford to a window. The lights from the windows sent a flickering illumination that made grotesque patterns on the courtyard below, and Rainsford could see moving about there a dozen or so huge black shapes; as they turned toward him, their eyes glittered greenly.

"A rather good lot, I think," observed the general. "They are let out at seven every night. If anyone should try to get into my house, or out of it, something extremely regrettable would occur to him." He hummed a snatch of song from the Folies Bergère.

"And now," said the general, "I want to show you my new collection of heads. Will you come to the library?"

"I hope," said Rainsford, "that you will excuse me tonight, General Zaroff. I'm really not feeling at all well."

"Ah, indeed?" the general inquired solicitously. "Well, I suppose that's only natural, after your long swim. You need a good, restful night's sleep. Tomorrow you'll feel like a new man, I'll wager. Then we'll hunt, eh? I've one promising prospect—"

Rainsford was hurrying from the room.

"Sorry you can't go with me tonight," called the general. "I expect rather fair sport—a big, strong black. He looks resourceful. . . . Well, good night, Mr. Rainsford; I hope that you have a good night's rest."

The bed was good and the pajamas of the softest silk, and he was tired in every fiber of his being, but nevertheless Rainsford could not quiet his brain with the opiate of sleep. He lay, eyes wide open. Once he thought he heard stealthy steps in the corridor outside his room. He sought to throw open the door; it would not open. He went to the window and looked out. His room was high up in one of the towers. The lights of the chateau were out now, and it was dark and silent, but there was a fragment of sallow moon, and by its wan light he could see, dimly, the courtyard; there, weaving in and out in the pattern of shadow, were black, noiseless forms; the hounds heard him at the window and looked up, expectantly, with their green eyes. Rainsford went back to the bed and lay down. By many methods he tried to put himself to sleep. He had achieved a doze when, just as morning began to come, he heard, far off in the jungle, the faint report of a pistol.

General Zaroff did not appear until luncheon. He was dressed faultlessly in the tweeds of a country squire. He was solicitous about the state of Rainsford's health.

"As for me," said the general with a sigh, "I do not feel so well. I am worried, Mr. Rainsford. Last night I detected traces of my old complaint."

To Rainsford's questioning glance, the general said, "Ennui. Boredom."

Then, taking a second helping of crepes suzette, the

general explained. "The hunting was not good last night.
The fellow lost his head. He made a straight trail that
offered no problems at all. That's the trouble with these
sailors; they have dull brains to begin with, and they do
not know how to get about in the woods. They do ex-
cessively stupid and obvious things. It's most annoying.
Will you have another glass of Chablis, Mr. Rainsford?"

"General," said Rainsford firmly, "I wish to leave this
island at once."

The general raised his thickets of eyebrows. He
seemed hurt. "But, my dear fellow," the general pro-
tested, "you've only just come. You've had no hunting—"

"I wish to go today," said Rainsford. He saw the dead,
black eyes of the general on him, studying him. General
Zaroff's face suddenly brightened.

He filled Rainsford's glass with venerable Chablis from
a dusty bottle. "Tonight, we will hunt—you and I."

Rainsford shook his head. "No, General," he said. "I
will not hunt."

The general shrugged his shoulders and delicately ate
a hothouse grape. "As you wish, my friend," he said. "The
choice rests entirely with you. But may I not venture to
suggest that you will find my idea of sport more diverting
than Ivan's?"

He nodded toward the corner to where the giant stood,
scowling, his thick arms crossed on his hogshead of
a chest.

"You don't mean—" cried Rainsford.

"My dear fellow," said the general, "have I not told
you I always mean what I say about hunting? This is
really an inspiration. I drink to a foeman worthy of my
steel—at last."

The general raised his glass, but Rainsford sat staring
at him.

"You'll find this game worth playing," the general said enthusiastically. "Your brain against mine. Your woodcraft against mine. Your strength and stamina against mine. Outdoor chess! And the stake is not without value, eh?"

"And if I win—" began Rainsford huskily.

"I'll cheerfully acknowledge myself defeated if I do not find you by midnight of the third day," said General Zaroff. "My sloop will place you on the mainland near a town."

The general read what Rainsford was thinking. "Oh, you can trust me," said the Cossack. "I will give you my word as a gentleman and a sportsman. Of course, you, in turn, must agree to say nothing of your visit here."

"I'll agree to nothing of the kind," said Rainsford.

"Oh," said the general, "in that case—But why discuss it now? Three days hence we can discuss it over a bottle of Veuve Clicquot, unless. . . ."

The general sipped his wine. Then a businesslike air animated him. "Ivan," he said to Rainsford, "will supply you with hunting clothes, food, a knife. I suggest you wear moccasins; they leave a poorer trail. I suggest too that you avoid the big swamp in the southeast corner of the island. We call it Death Swamp. There's quicksand there. One foolish fellow tried it. The deplorable part of it was that Lazarus followed him. You can imagine my feelings, Mr. Rainsford. I loved Lazarus; he was the finest hound in my pack. Well, I must beg you to excuse me now. I always take a siesta after lunch. You'll hardly have time for a nap, I fear. You'll want to start, no doubt. I shall not follow till dusk. Hunting at night is so much more exciting than by day, don't you think? Au revoir, Mr. Rainsford, au revoir."

General Zaroff, with a deep, courtly bow, strolled from the room.

From another door came Ivan. Under one arm he carried khaki hunting clothes, a haversack of food, a leather sheath containing a long-bladed hunting knife; his right hand rested on a cocked revolver thrust in the crimson sash about his waist.

Rainsford had fought his way through the bush for two hours. "I must keep my nerve. I must keep my nerve," he said through tight teeth.

He had not been entirely clearheaded when the chateau gates snapped shut behind him. His whole idea at first was to put distance between himself and General Zaroff, and, to this end, he had plunged along, spurred on by the sharp rowels of something very like panic. Now he had got a grip on himself, had stopped, and was taking stock of himself and the situation.

He saw that straight flight was futile; inevitably it would bring him face to face with the sea. He was in a picture with a frame of water, and his operations, clearly, must take place within that frame.

"I'll give him a trail to follow," muttered Rainsford, and he struck off from the rude path he had been following into the trackless wilderness. He executed a series of intricate loops; he doubled on his trail again and again, recalling all the lore of the fox hunt and all the dodges of the fox. Night found him leg weary, with hands and face lashed by the branches, on a thickly wooded ridge. He knew it would be insane to blunder on through the dark, even if he had the strength. His need for rest was imperative, and he thought, I have played the fox, now I must play the cat of the fable. A big tree with a thick trunk and outspread branches was nearby, and, taking care to leave not the slightest mark, he climbed up into the crotch. There he stretched out on one of the broad limbs and, after a fashion, rested. Rest brought up new confidence and almost a feeling of security. Even so zealous a hunter as General Zaroff could not trace him, he told himself; only the devil himself could follow that complicated trail through the jungle after dark. But, perhaps, the general was a devil. . . .

An apprehensive night crawled slowly by like a wounded snake, and sleep did not visit Rainsford, although the silence of a dead world was on the jungle. Toward morning when a dingy gray was varnishing the sky, the cry of some startled bird focused Rainsford's attention in that direction. Something was coming through the bush, coming slowly, carefully, coming by the same winding way Rainsford had come. He flattened himself down on the limb, and, through a screen of leaves almost as thick as tapestry, he watched. The thing that was approaching him was a man.

It was General Zaroff. He made his way along with his eyes fixed in utmost concentration on the ground before him. He paused, almost beneath the tree, dropped to his knees and studied the ground. Rainsford's impulse was to hurl himself down like a panther, but he saw that the general's right hand held something small and metallic— an automatic pistol.

The hunter shook his head several times, as if he were puzzled. Then he straightened up and took from his case one of his black cigarettes; its pungent incenselike smoke floated up to Rainsford's nostrils. Rainsford held his breath. The general's eyes had left the ground and were traveling inch by inch up the tree. Rainsford froze there, every muscle tensed for a spring. But the sharp eyes of the hunter stopped before they reached the limb where Rainsford lay; a smile spread over his brown face. Very deliberately he blew a smoke ring into the air; then he turned his back on the tree and walked carelessly away, back along the trail he had come. The swish of the underbrush against his hunting boots grew fainter and fainter.

The pent-up air burst hotly from Rainsford's lungs. His first thought made him feel sick and numb. The general could follow a trail through the woods at night; he could follow an extremely difficult trail; he must have uncanny powers; only by the merest chance had the Cossack failed to see his quarry.

Rainsford's second thought was even more terrible. It sent a shudder of cold horror through his whole being. Why had the general smiled? Why had he turned back?

Rainsford did not want to believe what his reason told him was true, but the truth was as evident as the sun that had by now pushed through the morning mists. The general was playing with him. The general was saving him for another day's sport! The Cossack was the cat; he was the mouse. Then it was that Rainsford knew the full meaning of terror.

"I will not lose my nerve. I will not."

He slid down from the tree and struck off again into the woods. His face was set, and he forced the machinery of his mind to function. Three hundred yards from his hiding place he stopped where a huge dead tree leaned precariously on a smaller, living one. Throwing off his sack of food, Rainsford took his knife from its sheath and began to work with all his energy.

The job was finished at last, and he threw himself

down behind a fallen log a hundred feet away. He did not have to wait long. The cat was coming again to play with the mouse.

Following the trail with the sureness of a bloodhound came General Zaroff. Nothing escaped those searching black eyes, no crushed blade of grass, no bent twig, no mark, no matter how faint, in the moss. So intent was the Cossack on his stalking that he was upon the thing Rainsford had made before he saw it. His foot touched the protruding bough that was the trigger. Even as he touched it, the general sensed his danger and leaped back with the agility of an ape. But he was not quick enough; the dead tree, delicately adjusted to rest on the cut living one, crashed down and struck the general a glancing blow on the shoulder as it fell; but for his alertness, he must have been smashed beneath it. He staggered, but he did not fall; nor did he drop his revolver. He stood there, rubbing his injured shoulder, and Rainsford, with fear again gripping his heart, heard the general's mocking laugh ring through the jungle.

"Rainsford," called the general, "if you are within sound of my voice, as I suppose you are, let me congratulate you. Not many men know how to make a Malay man catcher. Luckily for me, I too have hunted in Malacca. You are proving interesting, Mr. Rainsford. I am going now to have my wound dressed; it's only a slight one. But I shall be back. I shall be back."

When the general, nursing his bruised shoulder, had gone, Rainsford took up his flight again. It was flight now, a desperate, hopeless flight, that carried him on for some hours. Dusk came, then darkness, and still he pressed on. The ground grew softer under his moccasins; the vegetation grew ranker, denser; insects bit him savagely. Then, as he stepped forward, his foot sank into the ooze. He tried to wrench it back, but the muck sucked viciously at his foot as if it were a giant leech. With a violent effort, he tore his foot loose. He knew where he was now. Death Swamp and its quicksand.

His hands were tight closed as if his nerve were something tangible that somone in the darkness was trying to tear from his grip. The softness of the earth had given him an idea. He stepped back from the quicksand a dozen feet or so and, like some huge prehistoric beaver, he began to dig.

Rainsford had dug himself in in France when a second's delay meant death. That had been a placid pastime compared to his digging now. The pit grew deeper; when it was about his shoulders, he climbed out and from some hard saplings cut stakes and sharpened them to a fine point. These stakes he planted in the bottom of the pit with the points sticking up. With flying fingers he wove a rough carpet of weeds and branches, and with it he covered the mouth of the pit. Then, wet with sweat and aching with tiredness, he crouched behind the stump of a lightning-charred tree.

He knew his pursuer was coming; he heard the padding sound of feet on the soft earth, and the night breeze brought him the perfume of the general's cigarette. It seemed to Rainsford that the general was coming with unusual swiftness; he was not feeling his way along, foot by foot. Rainsford, crouching there, could not see the general nor could he see the pit. He lived a year in a minute. Then he felt an impulse to cry aloud with joy, for he heard the sharp crackle of the breaking branches as the cover of the pit gave way; he heard the sharp scream of pain as the pointed stakes found their mark. He leaped up from his place of concealment. Then he cowered back. Three feet from the pit a man was standing, with an electric torch in his hand.

"You've done well, Rainsford," the voice of the general called. "Your Burmese tiger pit has claimed one of my best dogs. Again you score. I think, Mr. Rainsford, I'll see what you can do against my whole pack. I'm going home for a rest now. Thank you for a most amusing evening."

At daybreak Rainsford, lying near the swamp, was awakened by a sound that made him know that he had new things to learn about fear. It was a distant sound, faint and wavering, but he knew it. It was the baying of a pack of hounds.

Rainsford knew he could do one of two things. He could stay where he was and wait. That was suicide. He could flee. That was postponing the inevitable. For a moment he stood there, thinking. An idea that held a wild chance came to him, and, tightening his belt, he headed away from the swamp.

The baying of the hounds drew nearer, then still nearer, nearer, ever nearer. On a ridge Rainsford climbed a tree. Down a watercourse, not a quarter of a mile away, he could see the bush moving. Straining his eyes, he saw the lean figure of General Zaroff; just ahead of him Rainsford made out another figure whose wide shoulders surged through the tall jungle weeds; it was the giant Ivan, and he seemed pulled forward by some unseen force; Rainsford knew that Ivan must be holding the pack in leash.

They would be on him any minute now. His mind worked frantically. He thought of a native trick he had learned in Uganda. He slid down the tree. He caught hold of a springy young sapling and to it he fastened his hunting knife, with the blade pointing down the trail; with a bit of wild grapevine he tied back the sapling. Then he ran for his life. The hounds raised their voices as they hit the fresh scent. Rainsford knew now how an animal at bay feels.

He had to stop to get his breath. The baying of the hounds stopped abruptly, and Rainsford's heart stopped too. They must have reached the knife.

He shinnied excitedly up a tree and looked back. His pursuers had stopped. But the hope that was in Rainsford's brain when he climbed died, for he saw in the shallow valley that General Zaroff was still on his feet. But Ivan was not. The knife, driven by the recoil of the spring tree, had not wholly failed.

Rainsford had hardly tumbled to the ground when the pack took up the cry again.

"Nerve, nerve, nerve!" he panted, as he dashed along. A blue gap showed between the trees dead ahead. Ever nearer drew the hounds. Rainsford forced himself on toward the gap. He reached it. It was the shore of the sea. Across a cove he could see the gloomy gray stone of the chateau. Twenty feet below him the sea rumbled and hissed. Rainsford hesitated. He heard the hounds. Then he leaped far out into the sea.

When the general and his pack reached the place by the sea, the Cossack stopped. For some minutes he stood regarding the blue-green expanse of water. He shrugged his shoulders. Then he sat down, took a drink of brandy from a silver flask, lit a perfumed cigarette, and hummed a bit from *Madame Butterfly*.

General Zaroff had an exceedingly good dinner in his great paneled dining hall that evening. With it he had a bottle of Pol Roger and half a bottle of Chambertin. Two slight annoyances kept him from perfect enjoyment. One was the thought that it would be difficult to replace Ivan; the other was that his quarry had escaped him; of course, the American hadn't played the game—so thought the general as he tasted his after-dinner liqueur. In his library he read, to soothe himself, from the works of Marcus Aurelius. At ten he went up to his bedroom. He was deliciously tired, he said to himself, as he locked himself in. There was a little moonlight, so, before turning on his light, he went to the window and looked down at the courtyard. He could see the great hounds, and he called to them, "Better luck another time." Then he switched on the light.

A man, who had been hiding in the curtains of the bed, was standing there.

"Rainsford!" screamed the general. "How in God's name did you get here?"

"Swam," said Rainsford. "I found it quicker than walking through the jungle."

The general sucked in his breath and smiled. "I congratulate you," he said. "You have won the game."

Rainsford did not smile. "I am still a beast at bay," he said, in a low, hoarse voice. "Get ready, General Zaroff."

The general made one of his deepest bows. "I see," he said. "Splendid! One of us is to furnish a repast for the hounds. The other will sleep in this very excellent bed. On guard, Rainsford."

He had never slept in a better bed, Rainsford decided.